WEDDINGS OF THE CENTURY

A PAIR OF WEDDING NOVELLAS

MARY JO PUTNEY

PANDAMAX PRESS

INTRODUCTION

Weddings of the Century includes two novellas, *Claiming His Bride* and *The Wedding of the Century*.

Claiming His Bride was originally published in a Signet historical romance anthology called *Dashing and Dangerous,* which is why the original title was the much more dangerous-sounding, *The Devil's Spawn*. But *Claiming His Bride* is much more appropriate because the story is about a young man returning after years of roaming the world to reclaim the young woman he's always loved—if she'll have him. This is the first time this story has appeared in a digital edition.

Dominick's story was inspired by the odd but true tale of Princess Caraboo. In 1817, a strangely dressed young woman speaking an unintelligible language convinced a town of people in Gloucestershire that she'd been kidnapped from her home in Polynesia and escaped her captors in the Bristol Channel, which was how she ended up in England.

She was much feted by the locals until a boardinghouse

keeper in Bristol identified her as an English servant girl named Mary Baker with a vivid imagination and apparently some experience with sailors from exotic places. Her story gave me the idea for Dominick's strategy in *Claiming His Bride*, and it was later the subject of a charming movie named *Princess Caraboo*.

The origin of the next story in this volume, *The Wedding of the Century*, was when I was delighted to be the first non-Harlequin author ever asked to contribute a long novella to a Harlequin historical romance anthology. The theme was "Brides," and what romance author doesn't love that topic? Inspiration for this story came from the real life marriage of the great American heiress Consuelo Vanderbilt to the 9th Duke of Marlborough. (Winston Churchill was the duke's first cousin.)

Blenheim Palace, the vast Marlborough estate, is near Oxford, England, where I lived for several years, and whenever I took visitors for the Blenheim tour, I saw the huge, splendid family portrait painted by John Singer Sargent. Consuelo was a beautiful swan-necked duchess, her husband looks very much like a duke, and the painting includes their two little boys and two dogs, but the marriage was not a happy one and ended in divorce.

I thought it would be fun to write a similar story with a happy ending. (Consuelo found happiness in her second marriage to a distinguished Frenchman.) I was aided in this by the marvelous book *To Marry an English Lord* by Gail McColl and Carol McD. Wallace. It's packed full of pictures and delicious details about American heiresses who married into the British aristocracy. (This is the same book that later inspired Julian Fellowes to create Downton Abbey.)

I liked the idea of finding two real people buried within all the celebrity trappings of such a famous and wildly publicized marriage. And then giving them a happily ever after.

–MJP

CLAIMING HIS BRIDE

CHAPTER 1

Devonshire, 1819

"*B*ut what if he refuses?"

Dominick Chandler silenced her with a kiss, which was what happened whenever she tried to be practical. Roxanne Mayfield sighed and relaxed into his embrace for a moment before pushing away. Trying to sound stern, she said, "Papa is not going to be persuaded by kisses."

Gray eyes sparkling, he brushed an errant red curl from her cheek. "That's all right. I wouldn't want to kiss him anyhow."

Trying not to laugh, she said, "Dominick, please be serious, we haven't much time. It was hard to convince Miss Bartholomew to let me see you alone for even ten minutes, and that wouldn't have happened if she weren't half in love with you herself."

His expression turned grave. "It's true that I've been a bit wild in the past, but I've never done anything really dreadful. My birth is good, I have a respectable income, and I'm reasonably eligible. Why would your father reject me? Here in the wilds of the West Country, there isn't a lot of competition for your hand."

She chuckled. "You mean he'll take your offer because I'm so hopelessly plain that otherwise he risks having me on his hands forever."

"Minx!" Dominick said appreciatively. "You know that's not what I meant. If you'd had a Season in London, you would have had half the men in England at your feet. But then you might not have met me."

"A thought too terrible to contemplate." For the thousandth time she marveled that such a splendid, charming, handsome man had fallen in love with her. But he had. Ever since they met by chance while riding, there had been magic between them. Roxanne suspected that she was the only person who really knew the honest, caring, vulnerable heart that lay beneath his dashing exterior. When she had recognized that, she had started to believe his declarations of love.

His hands tightened on hers. "I'm no paragon, Roxanne, but I swear that I will never fail you."

"I believe you." She shivered. "But I'm afraid, Dominick. You don't know Papa. He... He's not always reasonable, and he is not going to like the fact that you and I have been seeing each other without his knowledge."

"Since you spend all your time on the estate, how else could we have met?" Dominick said reasonably. "Granted, our courtship has been a bit irregular, but we've done nothing improper." He grinned. "I'm waiting for marriage for that."

She blushed and looked down, knowing how easily he could have seduced her if he had put his mind to it. She was lucky that he was honorable. But Papa was still not going to be pleased that she had a suitor. "If my father refuses your offer and forbids me to see you, what will we do?"

"Why, we'll run away and be married, my love."

Her eyes widened. "I couldn't do that! There would be the most dreadful scandal."

He arched his brows. "You wouldn't risk a scandal to become my wife?"

She bit her lip. What he was asking went against every principle of morality and propriety. To elope would be to carry a stigma for the rest of their lives. And yet ... Softly she said, "For that, I would dare anything."

His smile returned. "Then it's a bargain, my darling vixen. If your father refuses, we'll head for Gretna Green. You'll be the most lovely bride in Britain. Promise?"

Praying it would not come to that, she said, "I promise."

He gave her a last, lingering kiss, then turned to leave the drawing room so he could go to her father's study. As Roxanne watched him leave, a chill ran through her, a premonition that something would go horribly wrong.

Though her father was so absorbed in studying his bones and bits of pottery that he scarcely spoke to her, he did like having her around to order the household and write his letters. He hated change, and his first reaction would be to refuse any offer.

It wouldn't help that Dominick had a reputation for wildness and he was universally considered too handsome and charming for his own good. Yet Dominick was right that he was an entirely eligible suitor. In fact, he was something of a catch for quiet Roxanne Mayfield, if the truth be known.

Surely in time her father would come around. All they needed was patience.

Her hands clenched. And if patience wasn't enough, well, there was always Gretna Green.

🐚

*A*fter entering the study, Dominick spent several minutes shifting uncomfortably from foot to foot before he cleared his throat and said, "Sir William?"

The baronet lifted his head and stared balefully at his visitor. "Who are you and what do you want?"

Sir William Mayfield was a renowned student of primitive civilizations, and Dominick had assumed he was an absentminded scholar. But as he looked into Mayfield's cold eyes, he suddenly understood Roxanne's trepidation. This was not going to be easy.

He thought of Roxanne's sweet laughing spirit and warmth, her slim body and tantalizing red hair, the way she made him feel complete and happy, and he cleared his throat again. "Sir William, my name is Dominick Chandler, and I would like your permission to pay my addresses to Miss Mayfield."

Pure shock washed over the baronet. Leaning back in his chair, he said, "Of the Wiltshire Chandlers?"

Thinking it a good sign that her father knew of his family, Dominick said, "Yes, sir. My father was Charles Chandler, and I am heir to my uncle, Viscount Chandler."

His pale eyes like ice, the baronet said without inflection, "So you wish to marry my daughter. You're what, twenty-one or twenty-two?"

"Twenty-one, sir."

"And Roxanne is eighteen." With startling suddenness, Mayfield's calm manner erupted into rage. His face reddening, he snarled, "Do you seriously think I will allow my daughter to ruin her life by marrying a worthless, debt-ridden, dishonorable wastrel like you?"

Dominick stiffened, stunned by the virulence of the attack. Controlling his temper with effort, he said, "I'll admit that I've sometimes been intemperate, sir, but I'm not debt-ridden. I've inherited a competence from a great-aunt, and I'm about to take up an appointment with the East India Company. When my uncle dies, I'll inherit his title and a very pretty property. You won't have to worry about your daughter's future, sir. "

Mayfield leaped to his feet. Though he was inches shorter than Dominick, his fury made him menacing. "There has never been a Chandler worth the powder to blow him to hell! You're a bad colt from a bad stable, boy, and I don't want you near Roxanne! Do you understand me? I forbid you ever to see my daughter again!"

Dominick felt the blood drain from his face. Thank God Roxanne had already agreed to elope with him. That was not the way he had wanted to start their marriage, but if an elopement was necessary ...

Guessing his thoughts, Sir William growled, "Don't think that you can get around me, Chandler. I will discharge my daughter's worthless chaperone, and from this day forward she will not be allowed out of my house without two escorts. Men, not simpering females who might be taken in by you. Every servant on this estate, every laborer, will be told to give the alarm if you appear. The game-keepers will be instructed to shoot on sight. By God, I'll put man traps around the property! Step in one of those and it will cut you in half. You'll never see her again, boy! Resign yourself to that fact."

Dominick had aroused exasperation in many, and occasionally anger, but never anything like this. Bewildered, he asked, "Is it me that you hate, or would you feel the same about any man who wanted to marry Roxanne?"

"Both. My daughter is *mine*, and she belongs here at Maybourne. But it's a special pleasure to deny you. I knew and hated your father. He was just as handsome, just as selfish, just as arrogant, as you." Mayfield's face worked angrily. "He ruined the girl I loved! She killed herself after he betrayed her by marrying your mother, who was an heiress. I was never able to make him pay for his sins, and now he's beyond my reach, frying in hell. But the sins of the father are visited on future generations, and the good Lord has given me the opportunity to inflict a small measure of justice on you. I've waited many years for this moment."

A sick feeling twisted inside Dominick. His father had indeed been selfish and arrogant. He had abandoned his family for good when his son was seven, leaving behind nothing but a bad reputation that had tainted Dominick's life. Deeds that in most young men would be considered high spirits were considered proof of wickedness in Dominick. It seemed bitterly unfair that after doing so little for him in life, his father now had the power to cost him the girl he loved.

Hoping an appeal to reason might work, he said, "Is it fair that your revenge will cost your daughter her happiness?"

"Bah, *happiness*!" Mansfield sneered. "For a woman, satisfaction lies in service. I need Roxanne here to run my household and see to my comfort. It will be a better life for her than having her heart broken by a rogue like you."

"You're wrong!" Dominick retorted. "Roxanne and I love each other! We were born to be together, and you can't keep us apart. If we must wait three years until she is of age, we will. Since that is the case, you might as well consent now, and spare yourself alienation from your only child."

"'Born to be together! That's romantic rubbish." The baronet's eyes narrowed. "Your mother is still alive, isn't she? Do you want her to know the full measure of your father's wickedness? She's frail, I understand. Such news might be injurious to her health."

Dominick paled. "You couldn't be so cruel! She has suffered enough because of him."

"To save my daughter I would do far worse." The baronet paused, breathing heavily, before continuing with lethal menace, "If you ever try to see Roxanne again, I swear by all that's holy that I'll tell your mother every loathsome detail of your father's crime."

Dominick felt trapped in a nightmare. It had taken years for his mother to find a measure of peace after her husband's abandonment, and she had never regained her laughter. If she discovered that her marriage had been the cause of another girl's suicide, the shock might kill her. And if that happened--Dominick would never forgive himself.

Voice shaking, he said, "Very well, you win." He stopped as pain lanced through him. To give Roxanne up, to never to see the wondrous warmth in her eyes, or to kiss her welcoming lips... Never to introduce her to the mysteries of passion... Unable to see any alternative, he whispered, "I swear that I... I won't try to see Roxanne again."

"I want your word on that." Mayfield scribbled a few words on a piece of foolscap, then pushed it and a pen across the desk. "Sign this pledge that you renounce her, and I promise that your mother will never learn what your father did."

The paper said *I promise never to see Miss Roxanne Mayfield again*. Blindly Dominick lifted the quill, dipped it into the inkstand, and scrawled his signature across the bottom. It would have made more sense to slash his hand and sign in blood.

He turned and left before he broke.

৪১

*W*hile Dominick spoke with her father, Roxanne withdrew to her room and paced. The time dragged endlessly. Maybourne Towers had been named for the towers that stood at each of the four comers. Her room was in the southwest tower. Though the circular shape was inconvenient, she had asked for this chamber when she was a child because it made her think of fairy tales and princesses.

Yet though she had always loved the room, now it seemed a prison. Her perambulations took her to the west window. She glanced out over the park, catching her breath when she saw a dark-haired man riding away.

Merciful heaven, her father must have refused Dominick, or her beloved would not be leaving without seeing her!

He reined his horse in and turned around to stare at the house. Though he was silhouetted against the light and she could not see his face, there was a kind of wildness in his movements.

Roxanne waved frantically, but Dominick gave no sign of seeing her. The afternoon sunlight was reflecting off her windowpanes. She fumbled with the catch so that she could open the casement and call to him, but before she could unfasten it, he wheeled his horse and galloped away off furiously.

Driven by the greatest fear she had ever known, she

darted downstairs and went to her father's study. She took a deep breath, then went inside. "Papa?"

He looked up from his desk with a frown. "Yes?"

Clenching her courage, she said, "Did--did Mr. Chandler speak with you?"

"He did indeed. I'm deeply ashamed that you were so lost to decency as to engage in a clandestine relationship," her father said with icy fury. "Your precious suitor cost me half a year's income, but at least he's gone now, and good riddance."

The blood drained from her face. Refusing to believe the implication, she asked, "What do you mean?"

"He threatened to ruin you if I didn't give him money. He boasted of his power over you. That you believed every-thing he said. He wanted five thousand pounds to leave you alone, though he came down to a thousand quickly enough." Her father made a disgusted face. "It was worth that to get rid of him, but don't you dare believe the lies of another debt-ridden scoundrel. I can't afford a second affair like this."

She gasped, shocked to her core. "No, you're lying! Dominick didn't want money. He loves me!"

A contemptuous expression on his face, her father shoved a piece of paper across the table. "Oh? Read this."

She looked at the words scrawled on the page. *For a consideration of one thousand guineas, I promise never to see Miss Roxanne Mayfield again. Dominick Charles Chandler.*

Her vision darkened and she swayed on the verge of fainting. It couldn't be true. It *couldn't!*

Yet that was his signature, she recognized it from the notes he'd sent her. Charming, laughing letters, in which he had declared his love ...

Nausea swept through her. She had believed him. *She had been fool enough to believe him!*

In that instant her youth died. Setting the paper back on her father's desk, she said in a trembling voice, "It appears that I was mistaken in Mr. Chandler. I'm sorry for costing you so much, Papa." She swallowed hard. "It won't... happen again."

"See that it doesn't." Her father rose and gave her an awkward pat on the shoulder. "You're a sensible girl. You'll see, this is all for the best. In Wiltshire, his father was called the Devil, and young Chandler was called the Devil's Spawn. You're better off without him."

She gave a brittle smile before leaving the room. No doubt her father was right and this was all for the best.

But it was a pity that she hadn't died two hours earlier, when she had still believed in love.

CHAPTER 2

Plymouth Harbor, 1829

$\mathcal{A}$fter a nerve wracking climb up a wildly unstable rope ladder, Sir George Renfrew swung gratefully onto the deck of the *Lovely Lady*. To the nearest sailor he said, "I believe that Lord Chandler is expecting me."

"Right this way, sir."

Renfrew followed the sailor across the swaying deck, trying to remember when and where he had last seen his friend Dominick. It must have been five years ago, in Hong Kong. Or had it been in the Sandwich Islands? Somewhere exotic, at any rate, and that night they had become roaring drunk, making toasts to the good old days at King's College. He smiled reminiscently.

The sailor led him to a cabin door, then withdrew. Renfrew knocked and entered when a familiar voice called, "Come in."

Renfrew stepped into the lavishly furnished owner's

cabin. "Dominick, old man, how... " His voice cut off abruptly.

In the center of the cabin stood a hulking savage, his face obscured by wild black hair and a riotous beard. He was almost naked, with a crude whale-tooth necklace swinging across his chest and only a loincloth to cover his modesty. Hard muscles rippled beneath his bronzed skin as he stalked across the cabin, a guttural sound vibrating deep in his throat and a stone headed spear in his hand.

For a shocked moment Renfrew considered bolting. Reminding himself that he had bested Malay pirates in the South China Sea, he raised his cane and barked, "What have you done with Lord Chandler, you ugly savage?"

Amazingly, the brute began to laugh. "So I can deceive even you, George," he said in smooth, impeccably upper-class English. "That bodes well."

Renfrew gasped. "My God, is that you, Dominick?"

He looked closer and saw the familiar gray eyes. With a sigh of relief he lowered his cane. "Dare I ask what you are up to this time?"

Dominick waved his friend to the padded bench built against one wall. "I've come a'wooing."

George snorted as he sat and accepted a glass of brandy. "You've been away too long. If you want to win a wife in England, all you'll need is your title and the fortune you made trading in the East. You'll have to beat women off with a club." In fact, he thought as he examined the other man's powerful body, even the title and fortune wouldn't be needed. Women had always become buttery and wide-eyed around his friend.

"I don't want any woman, but a particular one." Dominick settled into a chair and regarded his brandy glass, his manner utterly at odds with his appearances

"Remember the family I asked you to gather information about? The Mayfields?"

Renfrew thought back. It had been over a year since he had made his quiet investigation and sent the results halfway around the world to his friend. "Ah, yes, the eccentric baronet and his spinster daughter. I wondered why you were interested in them." "Not them. Her," Dominick said succinctly.

"You want to court Miss Mayfield?" Renfrew said with surprise. "I've never met her myself, but by all reports she's a dry stick of a female. Hardly your type."

Dominick's eyes flashed. "Roxanne wasn't always a dry stick, I promise you!"

More and more interesting. Beginning to understand, Renfrew remarked, "Sir William is some sort of authority on primitive cultures, isn't he?"

"Exactly." Dominick swirled the brandy in his goblet. "From your report, Miss Mayfield never leaves the estate except in the company of her father. You also found that all letters go to Sir William, and he has long since discouraged her friends from calling." An edge of anger sounded in his voice. "She sounds very near to being a prisoner."

"I wouldn't say that," Renfrew objected. "She is merely a quiet woman who is devoted to her father."

"No," Dominick said flatly. "She's not really like that, but her father has given her no choice."

Obviously there was a story here, but it didn't look like Renfrew would hear it today. "What do you intend to do?"

His friend looked up. "Remember the strange case of Princess Caraboo, about ten or eleven years ago?"

It took Renfrew a moment to place the reference. "As I recall, she was some sort of East Indian princess who had been kidnapped by pirates, then escaped near the coast of

England and swam ashore, where she was taken in by a vicar and his wife. But she turned out to be a fraud, didn't she?"

"Correct. In fact, she was a poor Devonshire girl who spent time with the Gypsies, then married a sailor and picked up some Arabic and Malay from him. When he left her, she went off her head and started thinking she was a displaced Asiatic princess."

"An interesting tale, but what has that to do with you?"

Dominick grinned wickedly. "She became quite famous. Experts on primitive cultures came to study her and try to deduce her origins. People would have paid to see her, I imagine."

Renfrew's brows shot up. "You're hoping to lure Sir William Mayfield out to see you?"

"Exactly. From what you learned about the Mayfields, it would be almost impossible to communicate with Roxanne while she is at home, but Sir William would take her with him to investigate an interesting savage." Dryness entered his voice. "I gather that he needs her to take his notes and bring him tea."

"So you're going to walk into the middle of Plymouth dressed like that, and hope that Sir William and his daughter will come racing to meet you," Renfrew said with heavy sarcasm.

"Actually, I have a Polynesian canoe in the hold, and I'm going to paddle it onto a nearby beach." Dominick chuckled. "Let people think that I sailed her all the way from the Pacific. That will bring my quarry in a hurry. Sir William is particularly interested in ancient navigators, I believe. He had a variety of theories, most of them wrong."

"You don't look like any Polynesian I ever met. They don't usually run to beards, their features are shaped differently, and I certainly never saw one with gray eyes."

"How many Britons would know that? No one can prove that I didn't come from an island that hasn't been discovered yet." His eyes gleamed with mischief. "I'll give the experts a dash of Tahiti, a dollop of Sandwich Islands, perhaps a pinch of Samoa, and have them gibbering with confusion. "

"It might work," Renfrew admitted, "though you'll freeze if you prance around in a loincloth in this climate."

"I'll wear my feather cloak if I feel cold," the other man said blithely. "It's most impressive."

Renfrew's eyes narrowed. "'Fess up, Dominick. You didn't invite me here merely so I could admire your clever plan."

"Quite right." Dominick smiled wickedly. "There will be a stir when I'm discovered. Since you live in the area and have traveled widely, it would be quite reasonable for you to come see the wild man. I'll speak a garble of Polynesian languages, and you will profess to be able to understand some of what I say. With the distinguished Sir George Renfrew to certify my savage self, no one will doubt me." He stroked his wild black beard. "In fact, I shall become greatly attached to you and refuse to leave your side. You will become my keeper and protector."

Renfrew's jaw dropped. "Damnation, Dominick, I've turned respectable! Don't try to draw me into one of your mad starts. We're not at Cambridge anymore."

Dominick looked down his aquiline, un-Polynesian nose. "Not respectable. Stuffy. Hard to believe you're the same man who drove a herd of wild pigs through a Jamaican ball after the governor snubbed you."

"He deserved it." Renfrew tried vainly to repress a smile. "It was a most juvenile prank."

"But amusing." Dominick's face became serious. "This is

truly important to me, George. I will be eternally grateful if you help. You're the only man I can trust in such a scheme."

Suddenly uncomfortable, Renfrew stared down at his glass, swirling the brandy. He'd been in a bad spot once in Hong Kong, and Dominick had pulled him through it. His friend would not mention that. He didn't have to.

"Very well, I'll help if you wish," Renfrew said slowly. "But are you really sure about doing this? I gather that you fell in love with Miss Mayfield before you left England, but that was a long time ago. You're not the same person now. You may be setting yourself up for a crushing disappointment."

"Don't think I haven't considered that," Dominick said soberly. "It's true that we were both very young. But there was something between us that was timeless. I believe that it will still be there is I have a chance to meet Roxanne. I *must* do this."

Renfrew sighed. "Very well. Bring on the canoe!"

CHAPTER 3

Sir William Mayfield folded his newspaper and laid it next to his breakfast plate. "The coddled eggs were overcooked, Roxanne, and the braised kidneys were dry."

She glanced up from buttering her toast. "I'm sorry, Papa. Shall I order more for you?"

"There isn't time today, but see that the cook does better tomorrow." He peered over his half spectacles. "Fetch your bonnet and notebook. We're going to see a primitive curiosity."

It was typical of him to overlook the fact that she had scarcely touched her breakfast, but it was easier to obey than to continue eating. She laid down her knife and got to her feet. "Very well, Papa. What sort of curiosity?"

"A savage who appears to have sailed here from the Pacific."

"Is that the fellow they're calling the Wild Man of the West Country?" she asked with interest. "I read about him yesterday in the Plymouth newspaper."

"You shouldn't waste your time reading such rubbish. However, that is the nickname that the vulgar have attached to the brute." Mayfield permitted himself a thin smile. "Admittedly there is a certain logic to it. He is certainly wild, and quite unlike any creature ever before seen in this part of the world."

It might have been rubbish, but the story had intrigued Roxanne. "They say he's six and a half feet tall, that he sailed here all the way from Polynesia, and there's only one man who can understand anything of his speech."

Sir William sniffed. "Sir George Renfrew. The fellow is only a jumped-up merchant, but he sees fit to submit articles to scholarly journals on the basis of having traveled in strange lands. True scholarship is done reflectively, at a distance, uninfluenced by raw feelings."

As her father did. When was the last time he had experienced life firsthand? Repressing the disrespectful thought with the skill of long practice, Roxanne said, "I'll get my bonnet."

Upstairs in her room, she glanced in the mirror. An errant lock had escaped from the bun at her nape, so she secured it with the ruthless jab of a hairpin. It wasn't easy to persuade her blazing red locks to behave, but she persevered.

She was adjusting a navy blue shawl over her gray, high-necked gown when her gaze went back to her reflection. Her hands faltered at the sight of the sober, colorless, impeccably ladylike image in the mirror.

Suddenly, she was a stranger to herself. Where had the passionate, impetuous young Roxanne Mayfield gone? She was nearing thirty, and could not remember the last time she had laughed without restraint. Who was she to criticize her father for keeping life at a distance?

She drifted across the tower room. Though she tried never to think of Dominick Chandler, he still had the power to sometimes intrude into her mind. How many lives had he ruined in the years since he had destroyed hers? She gazed out through the west window. It was right there, by the beech tree, where she had last seen him, the sun behind him, silhouetting his broad shoulders ....

Her lips compressed into a harsh line and she turned from the window. She was fortunate that he'd displayed his wickedness to her father before she could ruin herself.

A thousand times over the years she had told herself how fortunate she was.

Throat tight, she picked up a notebook and headed for the stairs. Papa hated to be kept waiting.

It was a two-hour drive to Plymouth. As the carriage rattled to a halt in front of the Black Hart Inn, Roxanne said hesitantly, "After we've seen the Wild Man, can we drive down to Sutton Pool for a few minutes? I like to look at the ships."

"Nonsense, Roxanne, that would be a complete waste of time." Sir William climbed from the carriage and gazed at the inn. "The savage is being kept here, with Sir George Renfrew watching over him to make sure that he causes no trouble." He gave a rusty laugh. "Serve Sir George right if the brute murders him in his bed."

Roxanne failed to see the humor in such a prospect, but she could not suppress a tingle of anticipation as she followed her father into the inn. This visit was the greatest adventure she had experienced in years.

Inside, her father announced to the innkeeper, "I am Sir William Mayfield. Take me to see the savage, my good man."

The innkeeper gave a respectful bow. "Very good, sir.

He's in the assembly room. Several other gentlemen are observing him as well." He glanced at Roxanne doubtfully. "But I'm not sure the Wild Man is a decent sight for a young lady."

"Nonsense," Sir William said impatiently. "She's not a young lady, she's my daughter."

The innkeeper led them through the inn to a dim, high-ceilinged room where public dances and private banquets were held. Though the day was pleasant, a fire burned in the hearth, probably to give the savage the warmth he was accustomed to. Half a dozen men were clustered in the corner. In the center of the group, towering above them all, was a crested feather helmet.

Sir William marched confidently into the room. "Renfrew? I'm Mayfield."

A medium-sized man with blond hair and a pleasant face broke away from the group and came to meet the newcomer. "A pleasure to meet you, Sir William." His interested gaze moved to Roxanne. "Is this Miss Mayfield?"

"Of course," her father said, not bothering with a formal introduction. "Have you made any progress in discovering where the savage comes from?"

"Somewhere in Polynesia is the best anyone can say," Renfrew replied. "The fellow's language and customs don't accord precisely with any of the known island groups, though I can understand a little of his speech."

Her father ordered, "Roxanne, do a sketch of the savage's feathered helmet."

"His name is Chand-a-la," Renfrew said mildly.

Sir William shrugged. "A savage is a savage."

Roxanne bent over her notebook and did a quick sketch of the helmet. The man might not be six and a half feet tall, but from what she could see, he was well above average height. What had it been like to sail a canoe halfway around the world? How fascinating it would be if she could talk to Chand-a-la and learn about the wonderful things he had seen!

She gave him a quick glance. How strange and lonely he must find this northern land, so far from his sunny islands. She wondered if he would ever find his way home again.

Abruptly the Wild Man broke from the knot of observers and strode toward her, a velvety feather cape swirling lushly around his shoulders. Roxanne gasped, her gaze riveted by the expanse of naked bronze skin. The pattern of black hair across his chest and midriff paradoxically made him seem even more naked.

No wonder the innkeeper had had doubts about admitting her! She'd never seen so much bare male flesh in her life. His loincloth barely covered his--she groped frantically for a suitable word--his male parts.

Cheeks burning, she bent her head to her notebook and began to sketch the tooth-like ornament that hung around Chand-a-la's neck. He stopped beside her, his large, bare feet entering her field of vision. As she stared at them with a ridiculous amount of interest, a baritone voice crooned, "*Wahine*," into her ear.

"That is the Sandwich Island word for female," Sir George remarked. "It appears to mean the same thing to Chand-a-la."

Dark fingers reached out and stroked the back of Roxanne's hand. "*Nani*."

"That might mean pretty," Renfrew said thoughtfully. "Or perhaps soft."

The Wild Man must be warmer than an Englishman, for

his fingers seemed to scorch Roxanne. She edged backward, unwilling to lift her head and look into his face.

One of the onlookers murmured, "He's not so different from one of us. If I'd spent two or three years in a canoe without a woman, I'd certainly want to further my acquaintance with the first female who crossed my path." Someone hushed the fellow before he could say more.

Curiously Chand-a-la reached out, touching the brim of her bonnet. As if wanting to see her face, he said, "*Wahine*?"

"Behave yourself, you brute," Sir William said sternly. He raised his cane and shoved the tip into Chand-a-la's chest with bruising force, driving the savage backward. "Haven't you trained him to stay away from decent Christian women?"

Amusement in his voice, Renfrew said, "He's not easy to train, Sir William. But I'm sure he means no harm."

The Wild Man batted the cane away, saying in a voice of obvious disgust, "*Malahini okole*."

"Interesting," Renfrew said innocently. "In the Sandwich Islands those are the words for stranger and, er...,"he glanced at Roxanne, "backside. I wonder what they mean to Chand-a-la."

"Obviously something different." Sir William frowned at the Wild Man. "Is the canoe here? I'd like to see it."

Before Renfrew could answer, Chand-a-la said, "*Aole*!"

Unfastening his feather cloak and tossing it aside, he went to the fireplace and pulled out two burning brands. He raised the torches above his head, then began swinging them in an intricate pattern that blazed through the dimness like wheels of fire. At the same time he started shouting, "*Aie-yah! Okolemaluna-yah! Mahalo nui loa-yah!*" and similar phrases.

Chand-a-la's chant might have been an ancient ritual, or

it might have been nonsense syllables, but it filled the assembly room with a harsh, compelling rhythm unlike anything Roxanne had ever heard.

While the scholarly observers began scribbling madly, she simply stared, mesmerized by the sight and sound of the Wild Man. He was magnificent, surrounded by fire, a being of primitive, masculine power. To see him was to be carried away to a world far different from prosaic England.

Her reverie was interrupted when her father snapped, "For heaven's sake, don't gawk, Roxanne. Take notes. Try to catch the words accurately so they can be translated when we know more about his language. "

Reluctantly she bent her head, jotting a phrase, then taking a quick glance up before jotting another. Her cheeks colored again when she saw that Chand-a-la's loincloth was in danger of being dislodged by his energetic movements. Engrossed with his fire dance, he was splendidly unconcerned with propriety.

With a last booming "*Aie-yah*!," he hurled the burning torches into the fireplace, where they crashed in a shower of sparks. A collective sigh went through the watchers, as if acknowledging that they had been privileged to see a rare sight.

Even Sir William murmured, "Quite remarkable." His lips pursed as he noticed how bare the Wild Man was. "But the landlord was right. This isn't a fitting sight for a female." He took Roxanne's arm and started to usher her from the room.

"But, Papa," she protested, strangely unwilling to leave. "Surely you will need me for sketching and note taking."

"I shall manage," he said brusquely. "Tell the landlord to find a maid to walk down to Sutton Pool with you. I expect I shall that I shall be busy here for the rest of the day."

Chand-a-la was staring at her from the other side of the room. There was something about his posture that seemed familiar, but she could not place the memory.

With a sigh she turned to leave. Poor Wild Man, so far from home. She hoped the scholars treated him kindly.

CHAPTER 4

*D*ominick stared at Roxanne's retreating figure, unable to believe that she was leaving so soon, before he had a chance to speak with her and reveal his identity. Damnation, he had never even looked into her face!

She seemed so small, her movements and dress subdued, as if she were a docile wren. He needed to get her away from this place and these people so he could find the real Roxanne again.

He gave a wordless bellow and bounded across the room. Sweeping her up in his arms, he darted into the hall. A chorus of shouts rose behind them, but the longed-for feel of her slim body emboldened him. This time he would not let her get away!

Roxanne gave a strangled squeak as powerful arms swooped her into the air. Merciful heaven, the Wild Man was carrying her off! For an instant she was paralyzed with shock.

She began to struggle. Her arms were pinned to her sides, but she kicked out with her feet futilely, until she realized that she was exposing her limbs all the way to the knees. For decency's sake, she stopped thrashing. He couldn't possibly take her far, and she didn't sense that he intended to hurt her. He was simply curious.

As they whipped down the hallway, her gaze fixed on the small, delicately tinted shells that were woven into his beard. The effect was rather pretty. She had noticed that he didn't smell rank and primitive as she had expected. His scent was clean, with a hint of spiciness. Did savages bathe and use cologne the way civilized gentlemen did?

A customer was just entering the hall from the rear of the inn. As he gawked, open-mouthed, Chand-a-la shouldered past and burst through the door, bounding down the short flight of stone steps with a force that jarred Roxanne breathless.

The coach yard was deserted. Increasing his pace, the Wild Man bolted into the stables, his captive clutched against his chest. Roxanne felt numb with shock, the familiar scents of hay and horses totally at odds with this bizarre abduction.

With a flourish Chand-a-la set her on her feet, snatched a bridle from a nail, and unlatched the door to a stall. Then he guided her into the stall ahead of him so she could not escape. The bay gelding inside shifted nervously as the Wild Man deftly removed its halter, then slipped the bridle on.

Though Roxanne knew he could not understand, she said urgently, "Please, Chand-a-la, don't do this! There's nowhere to hide, and they might hurt you when they catch you." She placed a pleading hand on his arm. "Come outside with me now."

He glanced down at her hand, and she felt the muscles in his forearm tense. It was an odd moment that ended when shouts arose outside the stables.

He raised his hand and fumbled at her throat. She gasped and tried to retreat, stopping when she backed into the wall. Surely he couldn't be trying to molest her right here in the stable, when rescuers were just a few feet away, she thought wildly. But what did she know about how a savage's mind worked?

With a quick yank he untied her bonnet, tugged it off, and flung it aside. Then he brushed her head with a gesture that was oddly like a caress. Her hair loosened and fell in thick waves around her shoulders. His black beard shivered. Was that a smile behind the shrubbery?

He murmured a few words. Though it was hard to make them out because of the shouting outside, it sounded like, "Don't fear, *wahine*." But that couldn't be, since he didn't speak English.

Timidly she looked into his face for the first time. He was so tall and the stall was so shadowy that it was hard to see his features clearly. She did discover that his eyes were surprisingly light-colored, not black as she expected.

The door to the stable opened with a squeal of rusty hinges. Swiftly Chand-a-la lifted Roxanne onto the horse's bare back, setting her astride so that her skirts crumpled indecently around her knees.

Then he swung up behind her. Controlling the horse effortlessly, he rode outside, one hand on the reins and his other arm locked around Roxanne's waist as he brushed past the stable boy who had opened the door.

A dozen men were in the yard, several heading purposefully toward the stables while the others milled about in confusion. For a suspended moment everyone stared at the sight of Chand-a-la and his captive.

Sir William was in the midst of the group. Looking more irritated than alarmed, he barked, "There they are."

27

He began striding forward. "Unhand my daughter, you ignorant aborigine!'

An onlooker said with surprise, "Miss Mayfield's hair is quite splendid." Another man said admiringly, "For a savage, that fellow has a dashed good seat on the horse."

Ignoring the comments, Chand-a-la set the horse into a trot, heading for the arch that led to the street. A man cried, "Quick, kill the brute before he escapes!"

A portly gentleman who carried a fowling piece raised it and aimed at the Wild Man and his captive. As he pulled the trigger, Sir George swung his arm, knocking the barrel skyward as it discharged with a boom. "For God's sake, man!" Renfrew roared. "You mustn't kill Miss Mayfield while trying to save her!"

With acrid smoke filling the yard, the Wild Man put his heels to the horse and they broke into a gallop, whipping under the arch and into the street. Turning the horse to the left, Chand-a-la began galloping toward the outskirts of town as if the hounds of hell were pursuing them.

Roxanne clung to the gelding's mane helplessly as they swerved around drays and shrieking pedestrians. The wind whipped her hair free so that it lashed across her captor's chest. It was terrifying to ride without the security of a saddle. If it hadn't been for the firmness of Chand-a-la's grip, she would have been pitched to the ground.

She caught glimpses of white, shocked faces as they roared down the street. Dodging a woman carrying a child, the horse clipped a basket and rosy apples spilled out.

Dizzily Roxanne watched the fruit roll across the cobbles, then raised her head to see a pony cart loaded with hay blocking the street crosswise ahead of them. She gave a muffled shriek, sure a lethal accident was imminent.

Instead of swerving or pulling up, Chand-a-la set the

gelding into a suicidal jump. Even though she was convinced they were doomed, Roxanne automatically tightened her legs around the horse and held still so as not to throw the beast off balance.

They soared into the air, the Wild Man's body pressing against hers, keeping their weight centered over their mount's forequarters. A clump of hay tumbled to the street, dislodged by a hoof, but they landed safely. The Wild Man laughed with sheer delight.

Wherever he came from, they had to have horses, for he rode superbly. Roxanne turned her head and looked over her shoulder into his hirsute face. His eyes were gray, like those of ...

She went rigid with disbelief. No, it wasn't possible. *It wasn't possible!*

Chand-a-la. Chandler. The wretch! The bloody-minded, faithless wretch! The man who had broken her heart had returned.

And when they got to wherever they were going, she thought furiously, she was going to wring his neck.

CHAPTER 5

The sooner they got off the road, the better. Dominick couldn't have been more conspicuous if he had been painted scarlet. He kept the horse at a canter, hoping that he would remember the twists and turns that led to the cottage. During the days he had stayed there, he had come and gone by night and been heavily cloaked to conceal his wild appearance.

Luckily the cottage wasn't far, and it was approached by a sunken lane so no one was likely to see them during the last stretch. He was grateful that Roxanne seemed unafraid. A lesser female would be having strong hysterics.

He knew he should identify himself, but once they started talking, the explanations would be lengthy and possibly acrimonious. He preferred to remain silent a little longer. During a hard decade of traveling in the world's wild places, he had yearned for this moment a thousand times, and now he wanted to savor the wonder of her presence.

The cottage was set in the center of an apple orchard. It was the height of spring blooming, and the bewitching scent of blossoms hung heavy in the air as he pulled the gelding to a halt and dismounted.

When he lifted his arms to help Roxanne down, she came readily enough, sliding from the horse's back to land a foot away from Dominick. She really was a little bit of a thing, the top of her gloriously red head scarcely reaching his chin.

For a long moment they stared at each other. With ten thousand things to say, all he could manage was to ask softly, "Do you recognize me, Roxanne?"

"Of course I do, you idiot!" she snapped. "Have you lost your mind, Dominick Chandler?"

He laughed buoyantly. "I should have known that I couldn't fool you! I'm glad. You might have been frightened otherwise, and I certainly didn't want that."

"I find your solicitude unconvincing." Her eyes narrowed. "Having ruined my life ten years ago, it appears that you have come back to ruin my reputation as well."

He sighed as he thought of all the complications ahead. "I didn't plan it this way, but I thought that masquerading as a savage might help me get close enough to you to talk. I couldn't bear it when I saw you leaving, so I acted on impulse."

"I can see that you haven't matured any since I last saw you," she said acerbically. Taking the gelding's reins, she led it to a stump, climbed up, and tried to mount, but the stump wasn't high enough. After failing twice--and showing a delicious amount of leg in the process--she said, "Help me up. If I return to town quickly, it might be possible to salvage my reputation."

"Is that all you're concerned about? Your reputation?" He caught the gelding's reins. "I didn't go to this effort merely for the pleasure of running off with you for half an hour. We must talk, Roxanne."

"That's Miss Mayfield to you!" Standing on the stump put her eyes on a level with his. "There's only one thing I want to do with you, and it isn't talk."

Of course; he should have had the sense to kiss her right away. They could find each more quickly in an embrace than by speaking. He moved forward, eager to take her into his arms.

She hauled back her right arm and slapped him across the cheek with all her strength.

He rocked back on his heels. Eyes watering, he said, "You're angry over what happened."

It was her turn look incredulous. "Angry? That doesn't begin to describe how I feel!" For an instant her lip trembled. "The words don't exist, Lord Chandler."

"You know that my uncle died two years ago," he said with interest.

She looked away. "I noticed his obituary in the newspaper. Believe me, I was not following your inglorious career!"

But she had noticed, and remembered. "Come inside and I'll make a pot of tea," he suggested. "I imagine that we could both use some."

"*I* could use some tea. What you need is a shave, some decent clothing, and a sense of shame!"

She tried to rake him with a scathing glance, but her gaze faltered somewhere around his chest. He found her bashfulness enchanting. Taking the gelding's reins, he said, "I'll rub this fellow down if you'll start a fire and put the kettle on. I should be finished by the time it's boiling."

Not budging from her stump, she said, "Do thieves always take such good care of the horses they steal?"

He stroked the gelding's sweaty neck. "I didn't steal

Thunder. He belongs to my friend George. He's a fine fellow. I wouldn't have cared to try jumping that cart with a strange mount."

She hopped from the ground into the lush, ankle high grass. "You thought of everything, I see. Does the cottage belong to George as well?"

"As a matter of fact, it does." He led the gelding into the shed that leaned against the cottage. As he tethered it, he continued, "This is a remote corner of his estate. I stayed here for several days while we worked out the details of my plan. My baggage is still here."

She sniffed. "I'm surprised that you were able to convince a grown man to participate in something so childish."

Dominick grinned. "It took some persuasion, but once George agreed to help, he had even more fun than I did. What a stuffy lot those scholars were! It was amusing to lead them on."

Roxanne's hands knotted into fists, and she fought the temptation to hit him again. This was all just a game to Dominick. He was no more serious now than he had been ten years ago. All of her pain, all of her agonized, sleepless nights, had been wasted. She was a thousand times a fool!

Spinning on her heel, she marched toward the sunken lane. In two quick steps he was beside her, halting her progress with a hand on her elbow. "Where are you going?"

"That's a foolish question," she snapped. "Back to Plymouth. If I can't ride, I'll walk. It can't be more than four or five miles."

"No," he said flatly. His grip tightened on her elbow. "You are staying here until I've had a chance to say my piece."

Faint sun-baked lines bracketed his eyes. He looked

older, harder, and far more menacing than when she had known him before. For the first time she felt uneasy.

Well, she had changed, too. She was no longer the adoring, malleable female who had agreed with everything her sweetheart said. Jerking her arm free, she said, "You dare to hold me prisoner?"

He scooped her up again and carried her toward the cottage. "Having kidnapped you in front of an inn full of witnesses, I can hardly be in worse trouble than I am already."

This time there were no potential rescuers in the next room, and she fought for her freedom in dead earnest. He grunted when she drove her elbow into his belly, then jerked his head back when she clawed at his eyes. Her fingertips raked down his cheek, leaving red marks in the flesh above his beard. "Stop that, you little hellcat!"

She redoubled her efforts and for a moment she thought he was going to release her. Instead, he changed his grip, locking her arms by her sides. To her fury, he seemed more amused than upset. "It's good to know that my darling vixen hasn't been obliterated entirely," he said in a dulcet tone.

She caught her breath, unnerved to hear his old, loving nickname. Ceasing her struggle, she said in a voice that could have chipped ice, "I am not your vixen, darling or otherwise."

He turned sideways and ducked his head as he carried her into the cottage. It was a simple place, but clean. The whitewashed walls, rag rug, and well-worn wooden furniture had a certain homely charm.

He set her down again. "You can either walk into the bedroom, or I can carry you. What is your preference?"

She gasped, truly shocked. "So the purpose of your masquerade is rape?"

He looked startled. Then, as he realized how she had interpreted his words, he flushed scarlet. "Surely you can't think that I would ever force you!'"

Her eyes narrowed. "Raping my body would be a mere bagatelle compared to what you did to my heart.'"

The blood drained from his face, leaving him pale beneath his tanned skin. "I'm truly sorry for what happened, Roxanne, but I had no choice."

She retorted, "One always has a choice! The ones you've made do you no credit."

"Perhaps you're right," he said quietly. "But I did the best I knew how."

The pain in his eyes caught her off guard. This was the private, vulnerable Dominick with whom she had fallen in love. She vowed silently that she would not let him cozen her again, but she felt wry sympathy for Eve, beguiled by the serpent in the Garden of Eden.

Trying to conceal her weakness, she said, "If you're not interested in rape, why do you want me in the bedroom?"

"So I can lock you in while I rub down the horse," he said with exasperation. "I want to insure that you're here when I'm done, and the bedroom windows are too high and small for you to escape." He surveyed her. "Though now that I think about it, you might be small enough to get out that way. It will have to be the pantry. It's the only other door that can be locked from the outside."

Wordlessly she stalked to a door that opened from the kitchen end of the room. Seeing that it was the pantry, she stepped inside and slammed the door shut with a force that made the shelves inside vibrate. As he latched the door, she scanned her surroundings, glad that a high, narrow window let in light. The shelves were empty except for a few basic supplies and utensils.

A flash of reflected light caught her eye, and she saw that a small round mirror hung on one wall. She glanced in, and caught her breath.

Earlier in the day she had looked at her image and felt old and dull. The reflection that met her gaze now was entirely different, with snapping eyes and blazing hair rioting around her shoulders. She looked ... wanton.

The image was even more disturbing than the earlier one. She turned away and yanked her hair back into its usual knot. She had enough hairpins left to secure it, though only just. As the minutes stretched on, she wrapped her arms around herself, feeling the spring chill now that she was no longer in the sun.

Why on earth had Dominick abducted her? Certainly not for love, since he had never loved her. And in spite of the way he had hurt her before, it was hard to believe that he was simply being cruel, if for no other reason than that the effort involved was so great. The whole mad affair must be a product of his warped sense of humor.

Presumably he would release her soon, but nothing could prevent the story from spreading all over the British Isles. For the rest of her life she would be known as the spinster who was abducted by the savage. People would speculate in hushed, excited voices about what the Wild Man had done to her.

Would it be better or worse if it became known that "Chand-a-la" was an Englishman? Either way, her father would be furious at the notoriety, and he would blame her for it. She shuddered at the thought.

It was taking him a long time to groom that horse.

Her hands clenched as a horrible new thought struck her. Surely he hadn't become so angry that he would abandon her in this isolated cottage! He might be a wretch, but he wasn't a monster. Yet how much did she know about him? Nothing, really.

She found herself wondering how long it would take to starve. No, she would die of thirst first.

The pantry was just large enough for her to pace.

CHAPTER 6

*A*fter what seemed like an eternity, the door swung open. Roxanne bolted out, her relief boiling into anger. She was about to start snapping when she saw Dominick and her words died in her throat.

The Wild Man was gone. He had taken her at her word and shaved off the disreputable beard, trimmed his hair, and donned the impeccably tailored garments of an English gentleman. He must also have bathed and washed off some of the stain that had darkened his skin, for his complexion had lightened to a less conspicuous shade. No wonder she had been in the pantry so long.

Dominick made a deep, heavily ironic bow. "Is this satisfactory, Miss Mayfield?"

As a savage, he had irritated her. Now, as a gentleman, he terrified her. She had always known that his birth was higher than hers, but it had been easy to forget that when he had laughed and teased and coaxed her into loving him. Now he was the epitome of the arrogant, high-bred aristocrat.

Her jaw set stubbornly. She might be drab and

provincial, but she didn't have to admit it. "A great improvement, Lord Chandler." She sailed by him, head high, then settled in a Windsor chair and smoothed her skirts over her knees. "I believe you said something about tea."

The corner of his mouth quirked up, and he was no longer as intimidating. "As you command, Miss Mayfield."

With a flourish he produced an already prepared tray where a fat brown teapot steamed gently. Setting it on the table beside her, he said, "I believe this has steeped long enough. Will you pour, Miss Mayfield?"

She gave a prim little nod. "Very good, my lord."

Like the pot, the cups were simple cottage earthenware, but she poured the tea as if the service was porcelain. "There is no milk, but would you like sugar?"

"No, thank you, Miss Mayfield." Dominick took the chair opposite hers. He guessed that the excessive formality was appealing to Roxanne's sense of humor, for there was a glint of amusement in her eyes as she handed him a cup. That was a good sign. What a pity that she had ruthlessly pulled back her hair again. Ah, well, what went up could come down again.

He took several sips, then set the cup down. Now that the atmosphere was calmer, it was time to talk. "I gather that you never received the letter I sent you after ... that day."

She gave him a quick, startled glance, then looked down at her cup again. "I received no letter." Her voice trembled. "Though I can't imagine what you might have said that could have mitigated what you did."

Dominick was unsurprised to learn that her father had intercepted the letter. No doubt his servants feared the man more than Dominick's bribes could overcome. "It was not a brilliant example of epistolary art," he admitted. "As I recall, I said that I loved you, apologized abjectly for the fact that I had to leave, and promised that someday we would be together. Which is why I am here."

"So romantic," she said mockingly. "But words are cheap. What mattered were your actions."

His jaw tightened. It was time to stop protecting Sir William. "I don't suppose your father ever told you how he blackmailed me into giving you up. "

"He blackmailed you?" She slammed her teacup into the saucer. "Surely your memory is faulty, Lord Chandler!"

"Every word he said is engraved on my liver," he retorted. "Sir William said that my father, Charles, had seduced and abandoned the woman your father loved, and that she killed herself as a result. Your father wanted revenge, and he took it on me by swearing that he would tell the tale to my mother, who was in fragile health."

Dominick's jaw worked. "Believe me, it was the most difficult decision of my life. But as much as I loved you, I couldn't pursue my own pleasure when doing so would cost my mother her peace of mind, and possibly her life. If I had done that, I would not have been worthy of your love."

Roxanne stared at him. "A touching story. It might have convinced me, if I hadn't seen with my own eyes the paper you signed."

It took him a moment to remember. "That's right, your father wanted my renunciation in writing. I was so numb that I did as he asked, though I didn't see the point. The paper was only as good as my word."

He smiled humorlessly. "Which is to say, not good at all since I did not feel bound by a promise extracted by force. What kept me away from you was concern for my mother. When I learned that she was nearing death, I returned to

England to say my goodbyes." He drew a deep breath. "When she was gone, I was free to find you."

"Don't lie to me!" she cried, her face twisted with anguish. "You didn't give me up because you were a good son, but because my father paid you a thousand guineas to go away!"

He stared at her, staggered. "That's utter rubbish. There was never any mention of money. If Sir William had tried to buy me off, I would have laughed in his face."

Her hands locked together in her lap, white-knuckled. "I tell you, I saw the paper! Your signature was unmistakable. "

Dominick tried to remember back to what he had signed. When he did, he swore. "Damnation, your father must have added something! He wrote a sentence in the middle of a sheet of foolscap, saying that I promised never to see Miss Roxanne Mayfield again. I scribbled my name below. He could easily have added more."

Roxanne's face went white, leaving a pale, ghostly dusting of freckles on her high cheekbones. "No," she whispered. "*No!*" She buried her face in her hands.

His heart ached for her. He wanted to take her in his arms, but guessed that she would not welcome his sympathy.

At length she raised her head and said huskily, "It's your word against his. I don't know what to believe. Perhaps it no longer matters what the truth is."

"The truth always matters!" he said sharply.

She shook her head. "Perhaps my father did alter the paper you signed. Probably he believed that he was saving me from a disastrous marriage, and very likely he was right. We thought we were in love with each other, but we were children. What we felt was not love but the hot

41

blood of youth. We both would have regretted our rashness."

"No!" Realizing that he had shouted, Dominick moderated his tone. "Yes, we were young, but the love was real. No doubt we would have had ups and downs as all wedded couples do, but I would never have regretted our marriage, and I would have done my damnedest to insure that you didn't."

She gave him a twisted smile. "You really must be a romantic. But can you honestly deny that you've enjoyed your decade of adventuring? You must have done things, gone places, that would have been impossible with a wife and family."

He sighed. "You're right that I traveled wide and far, and there was much I enjoyed. But I went because I needed to occupy myself to numb the pain of losing you."

Her brows arched delicately. "Are you going to claim that you spent ten years without touching another woman?"

He hesitated, knowing that he must be ruthlessly honest if he was to win her belief. "There were women sometimes. I am not a saint, and the years were long. But I never loved another woman, and there was never a day when I didn't think of you."

"You weren't thinking of me, but an idealized vision of me," she said softly. "Give it up, Dominick. Reality can never match a dream."

She looked so somber, so unlike the Roxanne of his memory, that he almost surrendered. Perhaps she was right and he had been cherishing an illusion.

Then he remembered how she had been earlier, with her hair tumbled and her eyes blazing. She had been alive then as he guessed that she had not been for ten years. That passionate wench was his Roxanne, and by God, he wasn't going to lose her go for a second time!

He stood, looming over her. "If we give up without trying, Sir William has won, and I will not permit that."

She grimaced. "This isn't a contest between you and my father. Perhaps you're right, perhaps we would have made a success of marriage in spite of our youth. We will never know, for that time has past. I am not that girl, and you are not that young man." She got to her feet. "It's time for me to go. "

His eyes narrowed. "The only place you're going is Gretna Green."

She stared at him. "Don't be silly, Lord Chandler. You don't want to marry me, and I don't want to marry you. Don't try to hold on to the past from sheer stubbornness. "

"Don't tell me what I want and feel!" He caught her gaze with his. "We are going to marry, and we can sort out the wisdom of it afterward."

After a moment of appalled silence, she began to laugh. "Dominick, Dominick, you're absurd! Marriage is for life. It isn't like going into a shop, then leaving if you decide that the stock is not to your taste."

"This stock is very much to my taste." His slow gaze went over her from head to toes. She felt naked, embarrassed, and . . . aroused.

Suddenly alarmed, she said, "This particular lot of merchandise is not for sale. Take care, Dominick. Remember that this is England and try to avoid felonious crimes in the future."

She moved toward the door. He stepped around her, reaching the door first, then turned and leaned against the dark oak planks, his arms folded across his chest. "You're not going anywhere but Gretna Green." He frowned as he considered. "Though there is really no reason to go so far. You're no longer underage, so we can simply drive to London and get married by special license there. George can come and stand witness."

"This ceases to be amusing," she said in a dangerous voice. "Let me go, Dominick! I am not going to marry you."

"Why not?"

"Because...because the very idea is nonsensical!" she exclaimed. "We have nothing in common."

"It's true that men and women have little in common, but they keep getting married anyway." He smiled wickedly. "The few mutual interests they do have are usually enough."

She wasn't sure whether to laugh or blush. The sensation was familiar, for Dominick had always had that effect on her. For an instant she wondered what it would be like to be his wife. She felt an ache deep inside. To go to bed with passion, and to wake up with laughter ...

But it wouldn't be like that. Obviously he had cherished some romanticized image of her for the last ten years, and that vision was obscuring the plain, bread-and-butter reality of Miss Roxanne Elizabeth Mayfield, spinster of the parish. After taking a deep breath, she repeated, "I am not going to marry you."

"Yes, you are. You promised. Several times, in fact. Remember?" His face was amiable and ridiculously handsome. "We've been pledged to each other for ten years. It's time we marched to the altar. It will be a romantic tale, the wedding of the century!"

"For the love of...!" Clamping down on her exasperation, she said, "Very well, if you want me to make it official, I will. Any engagement that was between us is *over*. Am I making myself sufficiently clear?"

"Remember the discussions we had about Mary Wollstonecraft Godwin? You liked the fact that I supported the principle of equal rights and obligations for females. I still do. If a man isn't allowed to jilt a woman, then a woman shouldn't be allowed to jilt a man." He smiled angelically. "The betrothal stands."

CHAPTER 7

*R*oxanne gasped at Dominick's effrontery. "We are *not* betrothed! You can't force me to marry you. No vicar will perform a ceremony when the female is gagged and that's the only way you'll be able to prevent me from protesting!"

"Ah, but by the time we reach the vicar, you won't be protesting." His gaze holding hers, he stepped forward and drew her into his arms. Softly, gently, his lips met hers in a warm, thorough exploration.

She gave a tiny whimper and clutched his upper arms. His embrace was as familiar as her dreams, where he had come to her in the depths of a thousand nights.

The kiss deepened and he drew her closer. He was so tall, so muscular. She felt desire rising and her breasts ached with longing. With a gasp she tore herself away, unconsciously wiping her mouth with the back of her hand as if that would free her of his spell.

He gave a slow, dangerous smile. "You'll not escape me so easily, Roxanne."

She turned away from him, shaking. It wasn't fair that

she had to be reasonable for both of them! If it was left to Dominick, they would plunge into marriage, then make each other miserable. He would leave her, or take mistresses, and she would wish she were dead. If only she didn't love him ...

She stopped and pressed her hands to her temples. Oh, Lord, she did love him, didn't she? Against all sense, she felt exactly as she had ten years before. Even when she had hated him for his betrayal, she had never stopped loving him. She was an utter *fool*.

She must escape tonight when he was asleep, before she lost what remained of her wits. After swallowing hard, she turned to face him. "And you'll not change my mind easily, my lord."

"It will be interesting to discover which of us is more stubborn. We're well matched, Roxanne. That's one of the reasons I fell in love with you." His caressing expression turned pragmatic. "It's too late in the day to set off for London. I don't know about you, but I'm getting hungry. There should still be some food in the pantry. Shall we see what can be made from the supplies at hand?"

Having had ample time to inventory the pantry, she said, "There are eggs and potatoes and a knob of butter, so I suppose an omelet is possible. Perhaps there might be something useful growing in the old kitchen garden."

"Excellent idea." He ushered her outside. The flowering apple trees glowed in the late afternoon sun. "A lovely day, isn't it? England at its best."

She inhaled the blossom scented air, feeling the pulse of spring beat in her veins. She wanted to frolic like a lamb, careen as madly as a March hare. She hadn't felt so alive since ... since that magical season when she had fallen in love with Dominick.

Hastily she examined the long-neglected garden. "There are scallions over there, and a bit of parsley. They'll liven up the eggs."

"We'll have a feast." He knelt and used his pocketknife to cut the herbs. With a mischievous smile he added, "I'll peel and fry the potatoes. I'm not sure I should trust you with a knife."

"Wise man," she said tartly. "I might use it to cut out your heart."

Scallions and parsley in one hand, he straightened to his full height. "You don't need to do that," he said simply. "You already have my heart."

His gaze held hers, his gray eyes utterly without guile. She found that she was having trouble with her breathing. Perhaps ... perhaps it was really possible ....

She pivoted and headed back into the cottage. "I warn you, my cooking skills are indifferent."

"No matter," he said cheerfully as he followed her inside. "I have some French wine that could make stewed boots seem ambrosial."

Dropping all references to love, lust, and marriage, he removed his coat and waistcoat, then rolled up his sleeves and built up the fire. To her surprise, they worked together as smoothly as longtime dance partners, sharing utensils and taking turns at the table and the hearth. In spite of his comment about the knife, he passed it to her without hesitation when she was ready to chop the scallions and parsley.

For a gentleman, he was surprisingly competent in the kitchen. Deftly he peeled and cut potatoes, then fried the wedges into a crispy, golden pile. Feeling naughty, she stole one from the old chipped platter. It was hot and savory and delicious.

He grinned and ate a potato wedge himself, then

popped one into her mouth as if she were a baby bird. Her tongue touched his fingertips, tasting salt and sensuality.

There was an odd moment of complete, mutual awareness, and she feared that he could see the accelerating beat of her heart.

Nervously she turned and poured her egg mixture into the skillet. While she cooked a fluffy, fragrant omelet, he set the table and ceremoniously poured fine French Bordeaux into a pair of thick mugs.

She was folding the omelet over when he slipped up behind her and removed the pins that kept her hair in place. The whole mass tumbled down over her shoulders again.

She was about to scold him when he pressed a light kiss through the silky strands under her left ear, his tongue teasing the lobe. Her toes curled and she almost dropped the skillet. With a feeble attempt at severity, she said, "If you don't behave, your supper will end up scattered across the floor."

His lips moved down her throat. "If that happens, I'll find something else to nibble on."

Blushing, she slipped away from his embrace, then divided the omelet into unequal pieces and slid the larger onto his plate. The sun was setting as they took seats on opposite sides of the scrubbed pine table.

On impulse she raised her mug of wine. "To the past."

"And the future," he added immediately.

"The past is more certain." Nonetheless, she drank the toast.

Silence reigned as they applied themselves enthusiastically to their plates. Kidnapping appeared to sharpen one's appetite.

When he had finished, Dominick pushed his plate away

and leaned back in his chair with a happy sigh. "I've never had a better meal."

She eyed him askance as she neatly laid her knife and fork across her plate. "You undermine your credibility when you make remarks like that. If you say such ridiculous things about food, how can I believe the other things you say?"

Immune to the set down, he said, "I've had more elaborate meals, but plain food is just as good when it is well prepared." His warm gaze met hers. "And tonight the company is matchless."

Her gaze fell. Changing the subject, she said, "You made a very convincing savage. Were you imitating real aboriginals, or did you make everything up?"

"I blended the language and customs from different Polynesian islands. The largest part of my performance came from the Sandwich Islands, since I spent the most time there. On the other hand, the fire dance was from Samoa." He grinned. "After seeing one performed, I decided to give it a try and accidentally set my hut on fire. Everyone in the village was rolling on the ground laughing at me."

She had to laugh also as she pictured the scene. "What are the Pacific islands like?"

"Beautiful beyond imagining. The Sandwich Islanders ride giant waves on flat, narrow rafts, skimming the sea like birds. I tried that too, and almost drowned before I learned the knack. It was like flying."

His gaze became distant. "The flowers and birds are so brilliantly colored that they seem the product of a painter's opium dreams. Even the sands of the beaches come in different colors, from blinding white to shimmering black. And the volcanoes! Seeing one by night is a sight never forgotten. It was like looking into a rift that had opened to Hell. Where the molten stone flowed into the sea, pillars of steam billowed into the sky. It was truly awesome."

She exhaled, imagining the marvels he described. Correctly interpreting her sigh, he asked, "Would you like to go there for our honeymoon?"

She almost said yes before she managed to stop herself. "There can't be a honeymoon if there is no marriage. "

"You're a hard woman, Roxanne," he said, not seeming particularly worried. "Now that I think on it, it would be better to take you to the Caribbean. The islands are equally lovely, and a good bit closer. Turquoise seas, caressing winds. It's as close to paradise as one can find on this earth."

No, true paradise would be to live with a man one loved and trusted. Love alone was not enough. Trying to sound light, she said, "You should be writing travel books."

He grinned. "I considered it, but such tales should have a tone of high seriousness, and I could never manage that. It was my fate to always find the absurd instead of the sublime." He embarked on a hilarious series of stories about other misadventures in the East and the Pacific. Roxanne laughed more than she had in the last ten years combined.

As she sipped her third glass of Bordeaux, she began telling stories of her own. About the vague scholar who had visited her father with a coach full of bones, looking for help in assembling them into whole skeletons. About the gosling that had decided a dog was its mother, and the neighborhood lad who had run away to the Gypsies only to be sent back with the firm comment that they didn't need any more children, thank you very much, they had quite enough of their own.

Simple stories, but Dominick was amused. Mug

cupped in his hands, he lounged back in his chair, dark tousled locks falling over his brow. The giddy thought passed through her mind that perhaps love was simply a matter of finding someone who would always laugh at one's jokes.

She must stop thinking of love and start thinking of escape. Yet when she looked at him, her mind filled with images of how he had appeared as a nearly naked savage. His loose shirt, open at the throat, reminded her irresistibly of the broad, muscular shoulders beneath the fabric. The way his trousers pulled across his thighs made her remember how it had felt to be pressed against him. A male body was very different in shape and texture from that of a female ...

Mouth dry, she rose to her feet. He'd had enough wine so that he would sleep soundly, and she should be able to slip away. "Being kidnapped is fatiguing. I think I'll retire now."

"I'll help you make up the bed." He stood and led the way into the cottage's only bedroom. It was a cozy chamber, with a broad four-poster bed, a washstand, and a pile of expensive baggage along one wall.

Dominick opened the blanket chest at the foot of the bed to reveal worn but clean bedding. After the two of them had tucked sheets and blankets and stuffed pillows into cases, he said, "I'll join you in ten minutes or so."

Her heart jerked like a terrified rabbit. "I beg your pardon?" she said in freezing accents.

"Don't worry, I'll sleep on the floor, unless you invite me to share the bed," he said mildly. "But I really can't allow you to stay in the room alone. You might decide it's your duty to try to escape."

The beastly man could read her mind. She glared at him.

"So even though you claim to love me, I am your prisoner. Have you no shame?"

"I'm ashamed of many things, but not this. You aren't a prisoner. Merely a bride suffering a few qualms."

To her regret, she found that she had a lamentable desire to giggle. Schooling her expression, she said, "Be sure to give me enough time to prepare. Though it shouldn't take long, since I'll have to sleep in my shift."

"If you like, I'll give you one of my nightgowns, though you'll look like a snake about to shed its skin." After digging out a nightgown, he bowed politely, then left.

She undressed and washed, then donned the garment. He was right about the size; it was enormous on her. But the fine lawn fabric was soft against her skin, making her think wicked thoughts.

Everything made her think wicked thoughts.

She dropped a pillow on the floor, then added a couple of blankets from the chest. The pine planks didn't look particularly comfortable, but that was his problem.

After braiding her hair into a long plait, she slid into the bed and pulled the covers over her head. In the darkness, the unreality of her situation washed over her and her happiness leached away. The handsome, dashing man she loved wanted to marry her. It was a romantic dream come true.

Who would have thought that fulfillment of a dream could make one feel so wretched?

༄

Dominick allowed Roxanne time to settle herself, then quietly entered the bedroom. She was only a gentle mound beneath the bedcovers with not so much as a single auburn curl showing. He guessed that she was only pretending to sleep, but he didn't challenge that. After a lifetime of maidenly modesty, she was entitled to be nervous at having him so near.

Certainly her proximity unsettled him. How much would she protest if he joined her in the bed? His blood quickened. Though her mind might be doubtful, her body had welcomed his touch. It might take only a few kisses to persuade her to give him what he had dreamed of for a decade.

He was halfway to the bed before he managed to stop himself. It was bad enough that he was abducting her. He could not coerce her into an intimacy for which she was not yet ready.

Suppressing a sigh, he made up a pallet on the floor. He was unlikely to sleep much, so there was no chance she could sneak out without his knowledge.

In deference to his roommate's innocence, he donned one of his seldom-worn nightshirts. Then he blew out the candle, wrapped himself in the blankets, and tried to find a comfortable position. He would rather be in the bed ... but it was still heaven to doze off to the sound of Roxanne's gentle breathing.

CHAPTER 8

*D*ominick came awake with a start and lay still for a moment, wondering what had disturbed him. The moon had risen and cool, silvery light illuminated the room. But there was something wrong with the sounds.

After a moment he realized that Roxanne's breathing had changed. No longer smooth, it had become a series of faint sobs.

Stricken, he got to his feet and perched on the edge of the bed. Softly he asked, "What's wrong, my darling vixen?"

"Nothing." She made a choked sound. "*Everything!*"

He lay down on the bed and gathered her into his arms. Her small, curving body trembled as she hid her face against his shoulder.

"Why did you have to come back?" she said through her tears. "My life wasn't very interesting, but I wasn't miserable. Now I feel like a child pressing my nose to the window of a candy shop, yearning for something I can never have."

"What do you yearn for?"

"F-for love, for happiness, for laughter." She swallowed convulsively. "For you."

"Since you already have me, why are you crying?" he murmured as he smoothed back loosened tendrils of her hair. "I love you. I want to marry you and devote the rest of my life to pleasing you. Why is that such a terrible prospect?"

She began to cry harder. "How can I trust you?" she said haltingly. "You left me once. I'm a very ordinary woman. Once you realize that, you'll leave me again."

He winced. No matter how noble his reasons, he had left her. And once trust was gone, how could it be regained?

Perhaps if she understood why he loved her, she might start to believe in him. "Do you remember the first time we met?"

She gave a small hiccup. "Of course. I was out riding. You were looking for the ruined Roman villa near Maybourne and became lost and wandered onto our land. On that black horse of yours, I thought you looked like a magical druid prince."

He pressed a kiss against her temples. "You never told me that."

With a touch of her usual tartness, she said, "You already had quite a good enough opinion of yourself."

He shook his head. "Not really. It's hard to have a good self-opinion when everyone is convinced that one is going to the devil. My father had gone that way, and it was universally assumed that since I resembled him, I was equally damned. In some circles I was known as the Devil's Spawn." He had meant the words to sound light, but they came out edged with regret.

By her stillness, Roxanne had noticed. "Was your father that bad?"

He shrugged. "Bad enough. He wasted most of my mother's inheritance, had the reputation of a cheat at cards, and kept his word only when it suited him. When I was seven, he eloped to the Continent with a married woman. My mother never really recovered from his betrayal." Dominick took a deep breath. "I could overlook the rest but not that. She deserved better."

Roxanne's arm crept around his waist. "You never spoke of your father to me."

"Ten years ago I couldn't. Because I was young, it was very important for me to appear jaunty and unconcerned. I guess I was successful, but I felt as if there was a hole in the center of my soul. Then I met you. Riding through that clearing, your hair blazing like fire because you hated wearing hats." The image was as sharp in his mind as if it had been yesterday.

He ran one hand down her back. Under the thin fabric her flesh was warm and softly yielding. "I'd always enjoyed pretty girls. Usually I laughed and flirted a bit, then went my way without a second thought. But as soon as I saw you, I felt as if the hole in my soul had healed. I couldn't explain it then, and I can't now. Perhaps love can't be explained."

A little desperately, she said, "I can't help but fear that over the years you have built me into an impossible model of perfection. I'm no paragon, Dominick."

He laughed. "I'm well aware of that. You've a sharp tongue, a stubborn streak, and you see things perhaps a little too clearly for comfort. Yet at the same time, those are some of the qualities I love in you." He kissed her temple again. "Your intelligence." He brushed her lips lightly with his. "Your directness." He laid his hand on her heart. "Your warmth, and if you can come to trust me again, your steadfastness."

He felt the beating of her blood against his palm. "When I saw you today at the inn, I felt exactly the same sensation that I did ten years ago. That you, and only you, can fill the emptiness inside me. No one else has ever affected me that way, so I don't think you can be considered ordinary. Or if you are, perhaps ordinariness is what I need." He took an uneven breath, for honesty was painful work. "Certainly I need *you*."

There was a long silence before she whispered, "You make it easy to believe." Lifting her head, she touched her lips to his.

He responded with fierce sweetness, murmuring her name over and over as he kissed her. Her breath quickened and she did not object when he joined her underneath the blankets. It seemed so natural to have him beside her, to return his caresses and rejoice in his touch.

As passion claimed her, she forgot the long, empty years and pressed against him, wanting to feel the length of his body against hers. In the dark privacy of the bed, they might have been alone in the world, Adam and Even sampling the forbidden fruit of desire. The large nightgown slipped from her shoulders easily so that his mouth could simultaneously soothe and inflame the ache in her breasts.

Even so, she inhaled sharply when his hand slid beneath her gown and caressed the sensitive flesh inside her thighs. Hearing her alarm, he halted. "I have loved and wanted you so much, for so long, Roxanne," he said huskily. "I don't know if I can bear to wait any longer. If you want me to leave the bed, say so now, before it's too late."

For a moment, fear paralyzed her. She was standing on the edge of a precipice. If she dared to leap off into the abyss, her life would change irrevocably.

To accept him now was also to accept his offer of marriage and his version of the past. It would mean making herself vulnerable to the same kind of pain she had felt ten years ago, but it would be a hundred times worse if she lost him again after they became lovers.

And yet... She thought of the long, lonely years at Maybourne Towers, and had the stark realization that since that was her life, it was high time she changed or she would die without having lived. And he wanted her as no one else ever had. She was not a whim to him but a necessity, just as the memory of him had been necessary to her no matter how she had tried to deny it.

Feeling a deep sense of female power, she ran her fingers tenderly through his thick, silky hair. "You don't have to wait any longer, Dominick."

He exhaled roughly. Then, curbing his urgency, he initiated her into the mysteries of passion with infinite gentleness. She expected pain, and there was some, but there was also rapture beyond anything she could have imagined.

When she fell asleep in his cradling arms, it was with the greatest peace she had ever known.

*I*t was early when the laborer shuffled into the Black Hart Inn. "My name's Wussell," he said to the innkeeper. "Is this where the lady was stole from?"

The innkeeper winced. He'd never live this down. On the other hand, business was booming as people came to see the premises from which the Wild Man had abducted a modest English maiden. "This is the place. For tuppence you can see the room where it took place. Some of the savage's gear is still there." Wussell twisted his cap in his hands. "I'm not here for that. Yesterday I saw the brute and think I know where he might have taken the lady. They say her father is staying here?"

The innkeeper bustled off, and within five minutes Sir William emerged from a private breakfast room. "Searchers have been scouring the countryside without result," he said brusquely, "yet you claim to know where my daughter is?"

"Won't swear to it, but yesterday afternoon I caught a glimpse of a shaggy, naked brute riding with a lady in front of him." Wussell pondered. "She had red hair. Right pretty she was."

"A pity you didn't come forward yesterday, when there was still time to save her virtue!" the baronet snarled. "Heaven only knows what that savage might have done with her last night. She might be lying dead even as we speak."

Wussell shrugged. "Didn't know he was a savage. Thought he was just a member of the gentry being odd. There's no accounting for the gentry. Wasn't till this morning that the milkmaid told me about your daughter being abducted. Came as soon as I could."

"We must collect a party and rescue her," Sir William said. "Where is she being held?" Correctly interpreting Wussell's vague expression, the baronet dug into his pocket and produced his purse. "Will five pounds help your memory?"

"Reckon it would." Wussell accepted the money. "They were riding down the lane that leads to Orchard Cottage. This morning after I heard, I went to take a look. It's supposed to be empty, but there was smoke coming from the chimney, so I came here."

Sir William bellowed, "Innkeeper, find me some men! And make sure they're armed!"

❧

To go to bed with passion and wake up with laughter was even better than Roxanne had imagined. Dominick's head was pillowed on her shoulder and his arm draped over her waist. His face relaxed and peaceful, he was a bonny sight. It awed her to think that, God willing, they would be waking up like this for many years to come.

When she stretched lazily, trying not to disturb him, his eyes opened. There was wariness in the depths, as if he feared that she regretted what she had done.

Wanting to eliminate that doubt, she said teasingly, "I had no idea that it was so delightful to be ruined."

His tension disappeared and he gave her a smile that took her breath away, his gray eyes lucent with joy. "You're not ruined. You're better than ever. And so am I." His arm tightened around her. "I have trouble believing this is real, not just another dream. That finally we're together as we were always meant to be."

"In a dream, one isn't hungry, so this must be reality," she said pragmatically.

He laughed. "We'll have the rest of the eggs for breakfast. Then it's off to London for that special license. "

She made a face. "My father must be half out of his mind with worry. I really can't leave without telling him."

Dominick sighed. "I suppose you're right, but there will be hell to pay when he recognizes me."

She gave him a light kiss. "I don't expect that Papa will be best pleased, but he has no power to forbid me from marrying where I choose."

He kissed her back, not at all lightly. One thing led to another, and half an hour passed most enjoyably. Making love in the daylight had a special kind of intimacy. As he held her gaze with his, she breathlessly decided that she could grow very fond of it.

As they sprawled together in a tangle of damp, naked limbs, a shotgun blasted outside the cottage and a deep voice bellowed, "We know you're in there, Chand-a-la! Send Miss Mayfield out right now. If she's hurt, you're a dead man!"

Roxanne squeaked and sat bolt upright while Dominick rolled from the bed and grabbed for his scattered clothing. "Bloody hell, now we're in for it! I'm sorry, love, I didn't mean to pitch you into the middle of a scandal. We'll have to take that tropical honeymoon until the gossip dies down."

She dived from the bed and began yanking on her own garments, her heart pounding in panic. As soon as they saw her, every man out there was going to know exactly what she had been doing! Not that she was ashamed of her actions, but she would rather that all Devonshire didn't know.

Shotgun pellets rattled against the cottage wall, shattering a window. "Damnation!" Dominick swiftly pulled Roxanne to one side. "You'd better tell them you're all right, but don't stand in front of the window to do it."

Frantically she yelled, "Don't worry, I'm fine. I'll be out in a moment."

A familiar voice bellowed, "Is that really you, Roxanne?"

"My father!" she said with horror. Raising her voice, she replied, "Yes, Papa, it's really me."

Wordlessly Dominick fastened the back of her gown. His touch helped soothe her fear. She gave an unhappy thought to her hair, but if she delayed to fix it, the men outside might come in after her, and that could be disastrous.

She headed toward the front door. Before she could open it, Dominick took her hand. "We'll go out together."

She tried to disengage his clasp. "They might shoot you."

"They're looking for the Wild Man, not an English gentleman, so I'll be safe enough," he said reasonably. "Besides, I don't want to let you out of my sight ever again." He accompanied his words with a quick kiss.

Certainly he looked every inch a gentleman, not a savage. She was foolish to be so concerned. Yet she could not escape the fear that her newfound happiness was about to be shattered forever. Raising her chin, she led the way outside.

There was an instant of silence. Then her father roared, "Damn you to hell, Chandler! What are you doing with my daughter?"

When Roxanne flinched, Dominick murmured, "How nice to know that one hasn't been forgotten." Raising his voice, he said, "I've come to claim my bride after too long a betrothal! I hope you will wish us happy."

Face red with fury, Sir William stormed out of the shrubbery, several men behind him. "Wish you happy! You, you *criminal*! Did you hire that filthy savage to kidnap Roxanne?"

"Not at all," was the calm reply. "I *am* that filthy savage."

The baronet's jaw dropped as he stared at Dominick's face. When he recognized the eyes and features of Chand-a-la, he gasped, "You imposter! How dare you mock the scholarly pursuit of knowledge."

One of the searchers said with interest, "Well, I'll be, this gent here is the Wild Man." A murmur rose from the others.

Sir William snapped, "You lot get out of earshot. We have private matters to discuss."

With obvious reluctance, the other men withdrew and settled down to watch the show. Dominick waited until they were out of range, then said, "No subterfuge would have been necessary if you hadn't separated us for your own selfish reasons. But this time you will fail. My mother is dead, and there is nothing you can say to make me give Roxanne up."

Sir William appeared on the verge of explosion. Turning his attention to his daughter, he said, "Have you no shame? Allowing yourself to be seduced by this fortune hunter! Not only did he viciously extort money on the promise that he would leave you alone, but he has broken his solemn word never to see you again."

"A vow extracted under duress is not valid," Dominick pointed out.

Glaring, the baronet said, "What's your price this time? Since you've already ruined her, I won't pay as much as before, but it would be worth a couple of hundred pounds to get rid of you again."

"You never paid me a penny, Mayfield," Dominick said coldly. "I've told Roxanne the truth about how you falsified that document, so don't think you can deceive her this time."

For a moment the baronet appeared off balance. Then he said to his daughter, "You believed him? The man's a liar through and through. Having ruined God only knows how many other females in the last ten years, now he's back for another go at you."

"He loves me, Papa, and I'll not let you come between us." Though Roxanne's words were brave, Dominick saw that her fragile confidence was eroding under her father's bullying.

Sir William's contemptuous glance raked down her. "You're hardly the sort to catch the fancy of a man of the world."

"Don't speak to her that way!" Dominick snapped. "Any man would be proud to have Roxanne as a wife."

Despite his words, her face paled and her hand slipped out of his. Dear God, he was losing her! Even though her blazing hair still rioted around her small face, she was reverting to the meek, colorless woman who had come to the inn, and he didn't know how to prevent it from happening.

Pressing his advantage, the baronet said, "Have you no more brains than a goose? Chandler is after your fortune, for after I die, you'll be a considerable heiress. If you go with him, he'll live off your expectations. When he can't wring any more credit out of the moneylenders, he'll leave you flat. He's done it before, at least twice to my knowledge. Even if he goes through a marriage ceremony with you, it will be bigamous and illegal."

"No," she cried, horrified. "That can't be true."

"You're damned right it isn't!" Dominick said sharply. "I've never been wed, and have been betrothed only to Roxanne. For ten long years."

Simultaneously Sir William said, "It's all true, and more. I've followed Chandler's disgusting career for years." His lip curled. "Who are you going to believe? The father who has raised and protected you all your life, or a sly, deceitful rake?"

When her stark gaze went to him, Dominick said with anguish, "My God, Roxanne, after all that has passed between us, how can you not trust me?"

Her face mirroring the doubts warring within her, she said wretchedly, "I want to believe you, but...but I've never known my father to lie."

Dominick's eyes narrowed as he looked at the baronet. "On the contrary, he lies so well and so smoothly that I now wonder about the story he told me ten years ago, that my father was responsible for a young woman's suicide."

Ignoring him, Sir William said piously, "It's a sad day when a daughter doubts her father's word."

She pressed her hands to her temples, looking as if she was about to faint. She whispered, "Dominick?"

He shuddered and his hands clenched into fists. "I've

told you the truth," he said tightly. "It's my word against his, and you're going to have to decide whom you believe."

As she stared at him, paralyzed with indecision, her father put his arm around her shoulders and said in a gentler tone, "Come home, Roxanne. You've been a fool, but you're still my daughter. I'll pretend that this unfortunate incident never happened. We can go on the way we were."

As he tried to usher her away, she gave Dominick an agonized glance. His eyes were anguished, but he didn't try to stop her. He would not want a woman who did not have the courage to fight for his love as he had fought for hers.

She looked at her father and was sickened to see triumph in his eyes. He thought he'd won, and took more pleasure in defeating Dominick than he had ever shown in being a parent.

Which of the men had demonstrated love by his actions? Dominick, not her father, who had systematically undermined all her friendships until her life was as narrow as that of a nun. And which of the men did she truly love? Again, the answer was Dominick.

Wrenching away from her father, she said in a shaking voice, "I owe you a daughter's duty, Papa, but if you force me to choose between you, I choose Dominick!"

Unsteadily she turned to walk toward her lover. In two quick strides he closed the distance and swept her into his arms. "Dear God, Roxanne," he said hoarsely, his hand stroking her hair over and over. "I thought I'd lost you for good this time!"

"I'm sorry I doubted you," she whispered.

He hugged her more tightly. "Doubt is human. What matters is that you have the strength to follow your heart."

As she hid her face in his shoulder, she knew she had made the right choice.

But her father had not yet surrendered. "If you go with that man, you're no longer my daughter!" he shouted furiously. "I'll leave my fortune to the British Museum! See how long he stays once you're a pauper, and don't expect me to take you back."

"I don't want or need Roxanne's inheritance, Sir William," Dominick snapped. "Frankly, i think she would be better off if she never saw you again, but I shan't forbid her to communicate with you. It's up to you whether you have a relationship with her and any future grandchildren."

Heart aching, Roxanne turned to look at her father. Though he'd not been the most affectionate of parents, he was all the family she had, and it would hurt bitterly if he refused to ever see her again.

His face bore a desperate expression she'd never seen before. In a voice of raw anguish, he hissed, "Damnation, Roxanne, *this man's father eloped with your mother!*"

CHAPTER 10

*A*s Sir William's shattering words hung in empty air, Dominick gasped and his embrace turned rigid. "Dear God! But if that's true, why did no one ever tell us?"

Roxanne pulled away and pivoted to stare at her father, stammering, "It can't, it *can't,* be true! My mother died when I was four. I scarcely remember her."

Her father snarled, "The bitch didn't die, she ran away with her lover! Haven't you ever wondered why there was no grave?"

"I... I never thought about it. I assumed Mama was buried in Buckinghamshire at her family's estate." Stunned, Roxanne searched her memory, trying to recall what had happened. She'd looked forward to the nursery visits of her mother, who had the same red hair she'd bequeathed to her daughter. Sometimes she was charming and playful. Other times she was sad, with reddened eyes she couldn't disguise.

Then her mother stopped visiting. After what seemed like forever, Roxanne timidly asked when her mama would next come. The nursemaid said repressively that Lady Mayfield has passed on. There had been a strong implication of death, though the word had never been used. Roxanne had been too young to question further. And because she had lived such an isolated life, she had never heard any gossip to make her wonder.

Turning to Dominick, she asked, "You didn't know either?"

"I swear to God that I had no idea." He felt numb, and sure to the bone that this time the baronet was telling the truth. "One day my mother announced that my father had left us and would not be coming back. I didn't dare ask questions since the subject upset her terribly. She never mentioned him again except to tell me several years later that he had died in Naples. By then I had learned from a servant that my father had run off with a married woman, but I never knew her name."

"Well, you know now!" Sir William spat out. "My wife died at the same time, of the same cholera that killed your father. Yes, I lied to both of you when I forced you to leave ten years ago, but breaking up the relationship spared your mother the horror I felt when you asked for Roxanne's hand. Your mother would have been as appalled by a marriage between you two as I was." His face worked. "I've done my best to protect my daughter. I'd rather die than lose her to another Chandler."

Dominick stared at Roxanne, wondering what she was thinking. When she slipped away from him, he had the sick feeling that this time the baronet had won.

But he misjudged her. Stopping in front of her father, she said quietly, "The only way you will lose me is if you refuse to accept Dominick as my husband. He is not his father any more than I am my mother, and he is just as much a victim of their selfishness as you and I. Now I understand why you tried to separate us, but we are not the same as our parents. Dominick and I are both single and free to love each other."

With unexpected compassion for the older man, Dominick added, "Trying to deny our love will not change the past, Sir William. I'm sorry for what happened for all of our sakes, but I'll be damned if I will walk away from the only woman I've ever loved to pay for my father's crime."

His breathing harsh, the baronet buried his face in his hands. Gently Roxanne said, "It can't be easy to stop feeling anger after so many years, but for my sake I hope you will try. I don't want to lose you, Papa." She gave Dominick a quick glance. "We'll be going on a long honeymoon. When we return, I hope you will receive us at Maybourne Towers."

Sir William lowered his hands. His expression was haggard, but his eyes showed relief at having revealed his long-held secret. "Perhaps... by then I'll be able to. I don't want to lose you, either." With a flash of familiar belligerence, he said, "But if you make my daughter miserable, Chandler, I'll make you rue the day you were born!"

Dominick wrapped a protective arm around Roxanne's shoulders. "If she's unhappy, it won't be for lack of trying on my part."

After a hard look, the baronet gave a small nod, then turned and left the clearing. With a sweep of his arm he collected the men, who had been watching in fascination. A few minutes later hoof beats sounded as the would-be rescue party rode away.

Dominick gave a long, exhausted sigh. "Life is stranger even than I imagined."

Roxanne glanced up, her fox-brown eyes grave but serene. "It's not really such a coincidence. When we met, you said you were looking for that ruined Roman villa because your father had told you about it when you were a child. That is what brought you to Maybourne Towers. Perhaps the villa is what brought him to Maybourne and that's how he met my mother."

He drew her close. "It was wickedly wrong for my father and your mother to elope. Yet . . . if he loved her as much as I love you, I can understand why he did it. From what your father just said, they were together until death did them part."

"And if my mother loved him as I love you, I know why she left everything she possessed, including me, to go with him," Roxanne said softly. "I do love you, you know. I don't believe I mentioned that last night."

"You didn't, but we'll have ample time to rectify the omission." A smile in his voice, he continued, "Shall I take you to paradise for our honeymoon?"

"I'd like to see your islands, my love, but there's no need to travel that far." She burrowed into his arms with a sigh of pure joy. "I've found paradise right here."

Finis

THE WEDDING OF THE CENTURY

CHAPTER 1

Swindon Palace
Spring 1885

$\mathcal{A}$fter two weeks of dizzying social activity in London, a visit to the English countryside was an enchanting change of pace. Nature had cooperated by blessing the garden party with flawless weather. Puffs of white cloud drifted through a deep blue sky, the grass and trees were impossibly green, and the famous Swindon gardens were in glorious flower.

Yet the grounds were not half so splendid as the guests, who were the cream of British society. All of the men were aristocratically handsome and all of the women graceful and exquisitely dressed. At least, that was how it seemed to Miss Sarah Katherine Vangelder, of the New York Vangelders. As she surveyed her surroundings, she gave a laugh of pure delight.

The woman beside her said, "Don't look so rapturous, Sunny. It simply isn't done."

Sunny gave her godmother a teasing glance. "Is this the Katie Schmidt of San Francisco who scandalized English society by performing Comanche riding stunts in Hyde Park?"

A smile tugged at the older woman's lips. "It most certainly is not," she said in a voice that no longer held any trace of American accent. "I am now Katherine Schmidt Worthington, Countess of Westron, a very proper chaperon for her exceedingly well-brought-up young American goddaughter."

"I thought that we American girls were admired for our freshness and directness." A hint of dryness entered Sunny's voice. "And our fortunes, of course."

"The very best matches require impeccable manners as well as money, my dear. If you wish to become a duchess, you must be above reproach."

Sunny sighed. "And if I don't wish to become a duchess?"

"Your mother has spent twenty years grooming you to be worthy of the highest station," Lady Westron replied. "It would be a pity to waste that."

"Yes, Aunt Katie," Sunny said meekly. "If I'm very, very impeccable, may I view the rest of the gardens later?"

"Yes, but not until you've met everyone worth meeting. Business before pleasure, my dear." Katie began guiding her charge through the crowd, stopping and making occasional introductions.

Knowing that she was being judged, Sunny smiled and talked with the utmost propriety. She even managed not to look too excited, until she was introduced to the Honorable Paul Curzon.

Tall, blond and stunningly handsome, Curzon was

enough to make any woman gape. After bowing over her hand, he said, "A pleasure to meet you, Miss Vangelder. Are you newly arrived in England?" His question was accompanied by a dazzling smile.

If it hadn't been for her rigorous social training, Sunny would have gaped at him like a raw country girl. Instead, she managed to say lightly, "I've been in London for the last fortnight. Before that, we were traveling on the Continent."

"If you'd like to visit the Houses of Parliament, Miss Vangelder, I'd be delighted to escort you. I'm a member." Curzon gave a deprecatory shrug. "Only a backbencher, but I can show you what goes on behind the scenes and treat you to tea on the terrace. You might find it amusing."

"Perhaps later in the season Miss Vangelder will have time," Katie said as she deftly removed her charge.

When they were out of earshot, Sunny said with awe, "Mr. Curzon is the handsomest man I've ever seen!"

"Yes, but he's a younger son with three older brothers, so he's unlikely ever to inherit the title." Lady Westron gave a warning look. "Not at all the sort your mother wants for you."

"But as a Member of Parliament, he actually does something useful," Sunny pointed out. "My grandfather would have approved of that."

"Admiral Vangelder would not have wanted a penniless younger son for his favorite granddaughter," Katie said firmly. "Come, I want you to meet Lord Traymore. An Irish title, unfortunately, but an earl is an earl, and he's charming. You could do worse."

Dutifully Sunny followed her godmother to the next knot of guests, though she promised herself that she would slip off and view the famous water garden before she left.

Until then, she would enjoy the color and laughter of the occasion.

She was also guiltily glad to be free of her mother's rather overpowering presence for a day. Augusta Vangelder was the most devoted and solicitous of parents, but she had very firm ideas about the way things ought to be. *Very* firm. Unfortunately, she was laid up in their suite at Claridge's with a mild case of the grippe, so Sunny had the benefit of the more liberal chaperonage of her godmother. Not only did Lady Westron know everyone, but she made racy comments about them. Sunny felt very worldly.

While a courtly old judge went to fetch them refreshments, she asked, "Where is the Duke of Thornborough? Since he ordered a special train to bring his guests from London for the day, I should at least know whom to be grateful to."

Katie scanned the crowd, then nodded toward the refreshment marquee. "That tall fair chap."

After a thorough examination, Sunny observed, "He's almost as handsome as Mr. Curzon, and has a most distinguished air. Exactly what one would expect of a duke."

"Yes, and he's delightfully witty, as well," Katie replied. "Very prominent in the Prince of Wales's Marlborough House set. I'll introduce you to him later."

Sunny glanced at the other woman suspiciously. "Am I to be paraded in front of him like a prize heifer?"

"No," Katie said with regret. "Thornborough won't do. His taste runs to ladies who are .rather excessively sophisticated. He's expected to offer for May Russell soon."

"The American Mrs. Russell?" Sunny asked, surprised.

"Mad May herself. She's a good choice. Having had children by two husbands already, she shouldn't have any problems giving Thornborough an heir, and her fortune is immense." Katie gave a little sniff. "Heaven knows that Thornborough needs it."

Sunny's gaze shifted. "Who's the man standing to the left of the duke?"

Katie looked over. "Oh, that's just the Gargoyle."

"I beg your pardon?" Sunny glanced at her godmother, not sure that she'd heard correctly.

"Lord Justin Aubrey, Thornborough's younger brother, better known as the Gargoyle," Katie explained. "He manages the duke's estate, which means he's scarcely more than a farmer."

A line etched between her brows, Sunny studied the dark young man. While not handsome, his face had a certain rugged distinction. "Why was he given such an unkind nickname? He's no Mr. Curzon, but neither is he ugly."

"The Aubreys are known for being tall, blond and aristocratic, and Lord Justin is none of those things. He's always scowling and has no conversation at all." Katie smiled naughtily. "One would have to question what his dear mother had been up to, except that every now and then the Aubreys produce one like him. The youngest Aubrey daughter, Lady Alexandra, resembles him, poor girl. I imagine she's around here somewhere. She's known as the Gargoylette."

Sunny's frown deepened. "I'm sorry to think that these handsome people have such cruel tongues."

"They are no more and no less cruel than New York society," Lady Westron said dryly. "Human nature is much the same everywhere."

Sunny's gaze lingered on Lord Justin. Though not tall, neither was he short. He looked to be of average height, perhaps an inch or two taller than she. She guessed that he was in his late twenties, but his stern expression made him seem older. He looked as if he thoroughly disapproved of the splendid gathering around him.

Her thoughts were interrupted by Katie exclaiming, "Lord Hancock is over there! I hoped that he would be here today. Come along, dear, you must meet him."

After another wistful glance at the gardens, Sunny obediently followed her godmother.

⁂

The eighth Duke of Thornborough sampled a strawberry from one of the mounds on the refreshment table. "Splendid flavor." He reached for another. "You've been getting remarkable results from the greenhouses."

Justin Aubrey shrugged. "I only give the orders, Gavin. It's the gardeners who do the real work."

"But someone must still give the right orders, and it isn't going to be me." The duke consumed several more strawberries, then washed them down with champagne. "Relax, Justin. You've worked for weeks to make my fete a success, so you should try to enjoy the results. Everyone is having a cracking good time."

"That's fortunate, considering that this little event is costing over two thousand pounds." Money which could have been much better spent.

Gavin made an airy gesture. "The Duke of Thornborough has an obligation to maintain a certain style. After I marry May, there will be ample money for those boring repairs that you keep talking about."

Justin gave his brother a shrewd glance. "You and Mrs. Russell have reached a firm understanding?"

Gavin nodded. "We'll be making an announcement soon. A late summer wedding, I think. You can plan on fixing the roof directly after, so it will be right and tight by winter." He cast an experienced eye over the crowd. "I see that Katie Westron has a lovely creature in tow. That must be the Gilded Girl. I hear she's cutting quite a swath through London society. The Prince has already invited her to visit Sandringham."

"Then her social reputation is made," Justin agreed with barely perceptible irony. "But who is the Gilded Girl?"

"Sarah Vangelder, the fairest flower of the Vangelder railroad fortune." The duke's tone turned speculative. "They say she's the greatest heiress ever to cross the Atlantic."

Justin followed his brother's gaze to where the heiress stood talking with three besotted males. As soon as he located her, his heart gave an odd lurch.

Sarah Vangelder was the quintessential American beauty: tall, slender and crowned with a lustrous mass of honey-colored hair. She also had an engaging air of innocent enthusiasm that made him want to walk over and introduce himself. A beautiful woman, not his. The world was full of them, he reminded himself.

Aloud, he said only, "Very fetching."

"Perhaps I should reconsider marrying May," Gavin said pensively. "They say Augusta Vangelder wants to see the girl a duchess. Should I offer her the noble name of Thornborough?"

Justin's mouth tightened. Though he loved his brother, he had no illusions about the duke's character. "You'd find a young innocent a flat bore."

"No doubt you're right," Gavin agreed, but his gaze lingered. "She is very lovely."

Three peeresses and two Cabinet ministers came over to

pay their respects to their host. Justin seized the opportunity to escape, for the noisy chatter was driving him mad. He would have preferred to be elsewhere, but he could hardly avoid a party taking place in his own backyard.

Avoiding the formal parterre where many of the guests were strolling, he made his way to the rhododendron garden, which had been carefully designed to look like wild woods. There was a risk that he would find some of Gavin's fashionable friends fornicating beneath the silver birches, but with luck, they would all be more interested in champagne and gossip than in dalliance.

Half an hour in the wilder sections of the park relaxed him to the point where he felt ready to return to the festivities. Not that anyone was likely to miss him, but he liked to keep an eye on the arrangements to ensure that everything ran smoothly.

As he walked through a grove of Scottish pines, he heard a feminine voice utter a soft but emphatic, "Drat!"

He turned toward the voice, and a few more steps brought the speaker into his view. He was surprised to see the Gilded Girl. But that was too flippant a nickname, for the sunlight that shafted through the pine needles made her honey hair and creamy gown glow as if she were Titania, the fairy queen. He halted unnoticed at the edge of the clearing, experiencing again that strange, unsteady feeling.

A vine had snagged the back hem of Miss Vangelder's elegant bustled walking gown, and she was trying to free herself by poking with the tip of her lace parasol. Any other woman would have seemed ungraceful, but not the heiress. She looked playful, competent and altogether enchanting.

In the wooden voice he used to conceal unseemly feelings, he said, "May I be of assistance?"

The girl looked up with a startled glance, then smiled

81

with relief. "You certainly can! Otherwise, my gown is doomed, and Mr. Worth will be terribly cross with me if he ever finds out."

Justin knelt and began disentangling her hem. "Does it matter what a dressmaker thinks?"

"Mr. Worth is not a dressmaker, but an artiste. I'm told that I was singularly fortunate that he condescended to see me personally. After examining me like a prize turkey, he designed every ensemble right down to the last slipper and scarf." She gave a gurgle of laughter. "I was informed in no uncertain terms that any substitutions would be disastrous."

The vine was remarkably tenacious. As Justin tried to loosen it without damaging the heavy ecru silk, he asked, "Do you always do what others wish you to do?"

"Generally," she said with wry self-understanding. "Life is easier when I do."

Her skirt finally came free and he got to his feet. "I'm Justin Aubrey, by the way."

"I'm Sarah Vangelder, but most people call me Sunny." She offered her hand, and a smile that melted his bones.

She was tall, her eyes almost level with his. He had assumed that they would be blue, but the color was nearer aqua, as deep and changeable as the sea. He drew a shaken breath, then bowed over her hand. Straightening, he said, "You should not be here alone, Miss Vangelder."

"I know," she said blithely, "but I was afraid that if I didn't take the initiative, I'd leave without having a chance to really see the gardens."

"Are you rating them for possible future occupancy?" he said dryly. "I regret to inform you that my brother is no longer in the marriage mart."

"I simply like gardens, Lord Justin," she said crisply, her aqua eyes turning cool. "Are you always so rude?"

So the exquisite Miss Vangelder had thorns. Suppressing a smile, he said, "Always. I took a first in rudeness at Oxford."

Her expression instantly transformed from reproval to delight. "You have a sense of humor!"

"Don't spread such a base rumor around. It would utterly ruin my reputation." He offered his arm. "Let me escort you back to the fete."

As she slipped her hand into the crook of his elbow, she asked, "Could we take an indirect route? I particularly want to see the famous water garden."

He knew that he should return her before her chaperon became concerned. Yet when he looked into her glorious eyes, he found himself saying, "Very well, Miss Vangelder."

As they started down the pine needle carpeted path, he was very aware of the light pressure of her hand on his arm and the luxuriant rustle of her petticoats. And her perfume, a delicate fragrance reminiscent of violets....

He took a deep, slow breath. "I assume you are related to Admiral Vangelder?"

"You've heard of my grandfather?"

"It would be surprising if I hadn't." He held a branch aside so that she could pass without endangering her deliciously frivolous hat. "He was one of the great American success stories."

"Yes, and something of a robber baton as well, though he was always a darling to me. I miss him." She chuckled. "He liked people to think that he was called Admiral because of his magnificent yachts, but actually, he got the nickname because his first job was tending mules on the Erie Canal."

"Really?" Justin said, amused by her artlessness.

"Really. In fact, there are grave suspicions that his papa

was not married to his mama." She bit her lip guiltily.
"You're dangerously easy to talk to, Lord Justin. I shouldn't
have said so much. My mother would be horrified if the
Admiral's dubious parentage became common knowledge."
She grinned again. "Her own family has been respectable
for at least a generation longer."

"Your secret is safe, Miss Vangelder," he assured her.

She gave him another entrancing smile that struck right to
the heart. For a mad instant, he felt as if he was the only
person who existed in her world. She had charm, this gilded
girl, a quality as unmistakable as it was hard to define. He drew
a shaken breath and returned his gaze to the winding path.

Though she had said he was easy to talk to, in fact he
found himself talking more than usual as they strolled
through the park. He told her about the history of the
estate, answered questions about the crops and tenants.
Together they stood in the gazebo that was designed like a
miniature Greek temple, and when they visited the
picturesque ruins of an old monastery he described what
the community would have been like in its heyday.

She was a wonderful audience, listening with a grave air
of concentration that was occasionally punctuated by an
incisive question. After she asked about the effects of the
agricultural depression on the farm laborers, he remarked,
"You have a wide range of interests, Miss Vangelder."

"Education is something of an American passion. My
father insisted that I have a whole regiment of tutors.
Shortly before he died, he had me take the entrance exams
to Oxford and Cambridge. He was quite pleased when I
passed with flying colors." She sighed. "Of course there was
never any question of me actually going to a university. That
would have been shockingly bluestocking."

At least she had been well taught. Like most English girls, his own sisters had received the sketchiest of educations. Only Alexandra, who loved to read, had a well-informed mind. The man who married Sunny Vangelder would be lucky in more ways than one.

Justin had chosen a path that brought them out of the park's wilderness area right beside the water garden. It was an elaborate series of pools and channels that descended across three levels of terraces before flowing into the ornamental lake.

Sunny stopped in her tracks with a soft exhalation of pleasure. "Exquisite. The proportions, the way the statues are reflected in the pools, the way the eye is led gradually down to the lake. Masterful. And the grass surrounding it! Like green velvet How do the English grow such perfect grass?"

"It's quite simple, really. Just get a stone roller and use it on the lawn regularly for two or three hundred years."

She laughed and gave him a glance that made him feel as if he was the wittiest, handsomest man alive. His heart twisted, and he knew that he must get away from her before he started to act like an utter idiot. "I really must take you back now. Your chaperone will be worried."

"I suppose so." She took a last look at the water garden. "Thank you for indulging me, Lord Justin."

Their walk had taken them around three sides of the palace, and it was only a short distance to the Versailles garden where the fete was being held. As they approached the festivities, a tall man saw them and walked over swiftly. It was Paul Curzon, who had been at Eton at the same time as Justin. They had never been more than acquaintances. Curzon had been active in the most social set, while Justin had paid an unfashionable amount of attention to his studies.

After giving Justin a barely civil nod, Curzon said, "Lady Westron has been wondering what happened to you, Miss Vangelder."

Her face lit up at his words. "I was in no danger, Mr. Curzon," she said, her voice proper but her eyes brimming with excitement. "I'm an avid gardener, you see, and Lord Justin very kindly showed me some of the lesser known parts of the park."

In a careless tone that managed to imply that Justin was scarcely better than an under gardener, Curzon said, "You could not have chosen a better guide, for I'm sure that no one knows more about such matters than Lord Justin." He offered Sunny his arm. "Now I shall take you to Lady Westron."

Sunny turned to Justin and said with sweet sincerity, "Thank you for the tour, my lord. I enjoyed it very much."

Yet as soon as she took Curzon's arm, Justin saw that she forgot his existence. He watched them walk away together, two tall, blond, laughing people. They were like members of some superior race, set apart from the normal run of mankind.

For the first time in his life, Justin found himself resenting Gavin for having been born first. The Sunny Vangelders of the world would always go to men like Gavin or Curzon.

His aching regret was followed by deep, corroding anger. Damning himself for a fool, he turned and headed toward the house. Gavin's fete could progress to its conclusion without him.

CHAPTER 2

Swindon Palace
Summer 1885

Justin stared out the study window at the dreary
landscape, thinking that rain was appropriate
for the day he had buried his only brother. After
a gray, painful interval, a discreet cough reminded him that
he was not alone. He turned to the family solicitor, who had
formally read the will earlier in the afternoon. "Why did
you ask to speak with me, Mr. Burrell?"

"Though I'm sorry to intrude at such a time, your
grace," the solicitor said, "there are several pressing matters
that must be addressed without delay."

Justin winced inwardly. Five days of being the ninth
Duke of Thornborough was not long enough to accustom
him to his new status. "I assume that you are going to tell
me that the financial situation is difficult. I'm already aware
of that."

Another little cough, this one embarrassed. "While you are very knowledgeable about estate matters, there are, ah, certain other items that you might not know of."

With sudden foreboding, Justin asked, "Had Gavin run up extensive personal debts?"

"I'm afraid so, your grace. To the tune of...almost a hundred thousand pounds."

A hundred thousand pounds! How the devil had Gavin managed to spend so much? Justin wanted to swear out loud.

Seeing his expression, Mr. Burrell said, "It was unfortunate that your brother's death occurred just when it did."

"You mean the fact that he died while on his way to marry May Russell? It certainly would have been more prudent to have waited until after the wedding," Justin said bitterly.

It would have been even more prudent if Gavin had stayed in the private Thornborough railway car. Instead, he had been taken by the charms of a French lady and had gone to her compartment. When the train crashed, the duke and his inamorata had both died, locked in a scandalous embrace. If Gavin had been in his own car, he would have survived the crash with scarcely a bruise.

Oh, damn, Gavin, why did you have to get yourself killed?

Justin swallowed hard. "Obviously drastic measures will be required to save the family from bankruptcy."

"You could sell some land."

"No!" More moderately, Justin said, "The land is held in trust for future generations. It should not be sold to pay frivolous debts."

Burrell nodded, as if he had expected that response. "The only other choice is for you to make an advantageous marriage."

"Become a fortune hunter, you mean?"

"It's a time-honored tradition, your grace," Burrell pointed out with dignity. "You have a great deal to offer a well-dowered bride. One of England's greatest names, and the most magnificent private palace in Great Britain."

"A palace whose roof leaks," Justin said dryly. "Even as we speak, dozens of buckets in the attic are filling with water."

"In that case, the sooner you marry, the better." The solicitor cleared his throat with a new intonation. "In fact, Mrs. Russell hinted to me this morning that if you were interested in contracting an alliance with her, she would look with favor on your suit."

"Marry my brother's fiancée?" Justin said incredulously. He thought of how May had looked earlier at Gavin's funeral, weeping copiously, her beautiful face obscured by her black mourning veil. Perhaps if he had looked more closely, he would have seen a speculative gleam in her eyes. "It's hard to believe that even she would go to such lengths to become a duchess."

"The lady implied that she has a certain fondness for you as well," Burrell said piously.

"The lady has a deficient memory," Justin retorted. It was May Russell who had first called him the Gargoyle. She had been demonstrating her wittiness. Even Gavin had laughed.

"She has a very large fortune under her own control," the solicitor said with regret. "But I suppose you're right, it would be unseemly for you to marry your brother's betrothed. Do you have another suitable female in mind?"

"No, for the last several years, I've been too busy to look for a wife." Justin returned to his position by the window and stared blindly across the grounds. Burrell was right that marriage was the only plausible answer. Justin wouldn't be the first, and certainly not the last, to marry for money.

Even as a younger son, Justin would have had no trouble finding a wife, for he was an Aubrey, had no appalling vices and he had inherited an adequate private income. Yet though Gavin's entertaining had brought a steady stream of polished, fashionable females through Swindon, there had never been one whom Justin had wanted for a wife.

Except...

He closed his eyes, and instantly the memory he had tried to suppress for months crossed his mind. A perfect spring day, a tall, graceful young woman with a smile of such bright sweetness that she was nicknamed for the sun. The image was more real than the foggy landscape outside.

Though Justin had hated himself for his weakness, he had compulsively tracked Sunny Vangelder's triumphant passage through English society. Scarcely an issue of the *Morning Post* had arrived without mentioning her presentation at court, or her glowing appearance at a ball, or the fact that she had been seen riding in Rotten Row. Rumor said that many men had asked for her hand, and daily Justin had steeled himself for an announcement of a brilliant match. Yet at the end of the season, she had left London still unbetrothed.

He drew a painful breath. It was absurd to think of such an incomparable female marrying someone as ordinary as himself. But Gavin had said that she was the greatest heiress ever to cross the Atlantic, which meant that she was exactly the sort of wife Justin needed. And it was also said that her mother wanted to see her a duchess.

Scarcely daring to hope, he asked, "Do you know if Miss Vangelder has contracted a marriage yet?"

"You want to marry the Gilded Girl?" Burrell said,

unable to conceal his shock at such effrontery. "Winning her would be quite a coup, but difficult, very difficult. There's a mining heiress from San Francisco who might be a better choice. Almost as wealthy, and I am acquainted with her father. Or perhaps..."

Interrupting the solicitor, Justin said, "I would prefer Miss Vangelder. I met her once, and found her...very amiable."

After a long pause, Burrell said doubtfully, "Of course, you are the Duke of Thornborough. Perhaps it could be done."

Justin smiled humorlessly at the slate-gray pools of the water garden. "How does one go about selling oneself, Burrell? My experience is sadly deficient."

Ignoring the sardonic tone, the solicitor said, "I shall visit Lady Westron. She's the girl's godmother, you know. If she thinks the idea has merit, she can write Augusta Vangelder."

"Then by all means call on her ladyship before the roof collapses."

"There is one thing you should consider before proceeding, your grace," Burrell said with a warning note. "There are more American heiresses than English ones, and they tend to be much more polished, but a drawback of such an alliance is that the families usually drive hard bargains. You would probably have restrictions placed on your control of the dowry, and you might have to return the balance if the marriage ends."

Justin's mouth tightened. "I wouldn't be marrying the girl with the intention of divorcing her, Burrell."

"Of course not," the solicitor said quickly. After a shuffle of papers, he added, "If I may say so, you're very different from your brother."

"Say what you like," Justin said tersely. Yet though he told himself that a rich wife was strictly a practical matter, the possibility of marrying Sunny Vangelder filled him with raw, aching hunger.

If she came to Swindon, there would always be sunshine.

🍂

Newport, Rhode Island

*L*aughing and breathless from the bicycle ride, Sunny waved goodbye to her friends, then skipped up the steps of The Tides, the Vangelder summer home. Like most Newport "cottages," it would have been called a mansion anywhere else. But the atmosphere was more relaxed than New York City and she always enjoyed the months spent in Newport.

This summer was the best ever, because the Honorable Paul Curzon was visiting the Astors. He had arrived in Newport three weeks earlier, and the first time they had waltzed together he had confided that he had come to America to see Sunny.

She had almost expired from sheer bliss, for she had been thinking of Paul ever since their first meeting. They had carried on a delicious flirtation throughout the season, and she had sensed that there were deeper feelings on both sides. She'd been bitterly disappointed that he had not offered for her then.

As they danced, he explained that he had not spoken earlier for he had feared that he would not be considered an acceptable suitor. But after weeks of yearning, he had finally decided to come to America and declare his love.

Breathlessly she had confessed that she also had tender

feelings for him. Ever since that night, she had been living in an enchanted dream. Each morning she woke with the knowledge that she would see Paul at least once during the day, perhaps more than that. The business of Newport was society, and there was an endless succession of balls and dinner parties and polo matches.

Though the two of them had behaved impeccably in public, on two magical occasions they had had a moment's privacy, and he had kissed her with a passion that made her blood sing through her veins. At night, as she lay in her chaste bed, she remembered those kisses and yearned for more.

His courtship had culminated this morning, in the few minutes when the two of them had cycled ahead of the rest of their party. After declaring his love, he had asked her to marry him. Dizzy with delight, she had accepted instantly.

As Sunny stepped into the cool marble vestibule of The Tides, she tried to calm her expression, for she knew that she was beaming like a fool. It was going to be hard to keep her lovely secret, but she must until the next day, when Paul would ask her mother's permission. Her mother would not be enthralled by the match, but Sunny was sure she would come around. Paul came from a fine family and he had a distinguished career in front of him.

She handed the butler her hat, saying gaily, "It's a beautiful day, Graves."

"Indeed it is, Miss Sarah." Taking the hat, he added, "Your mother has asked that you see her as soon as you return home. I believe that she is in her private salon."

Such summons were not uncommon, so Sunny went upstairs with no premonition of disaster. She knocked on her mother's door and was invited in.

When she entered, Augusta looked up from her desk

with triumph in her eyes. "I have splendid news, Sarah! I'll admit I was tempted by some of the offers I received for your hand, but it was right to wait." After a portentous pause, she said, "You, my dear, are going to become the Duchess of Thornborough."

The shock was so stunning that at first Sunny could only say stupidly, "What on earth do you mean?"

"You're going to marry Thornborough, of course," her mother said briskly. "For the last several days cables have been flying back and forth between Newport and England. The essentials have been settled, and Thornborough is on his way to Newport to make you a formal offer."

"But I thought the Duke of Thornborough was going to marry Mrs. Russell."

"That was Gavin, the eighth duke. Unfortunately he was killed in a train wreck several weeks ago, two days before he was to marry May." Augusta smiled maliciously. "I would wager that May tried her luck with his successor, but clearly the ninth duke has better taste than his brother."

Feeling ice-cold, Sunny sank into a chair. "How can I marry a man whom I've never even met?" she said weakly.

"Katie Westron said that you did meet him. In fact, you spent a rather indecent amount of time strolling through the Swindon gardens together," her mother said. "He was Lord Justin Aubrey then, younger brother to the duke who just died."

The fete at Swindon was when Sunny had met Paul. Beside that, other events of the day had paled. Dazedly she tried to remember more. The gardens had been superb, and she vaguely recalled being escorted through them by some- one. Had that been Lord Justin? She supposed so, though she could remember nothing about him except that he was dark, and quiet, and...unmemorable.

But it didn't matter what he was like, because she wasn't going to marry him. Steeling herself for battle, Sunny said, "I can't marry Thornborough because I'm betrothed to Paul Curzon."

There was an instant of ominous silence before her mother exploded. "Nonsense! I considered putting a stop to that earlier, but I thought it was a harmless flirtation. I couldn't believe you would be so foolish as to entertain thoughts of marrying such a man." Her eyes narrowed. "I trust you've had the sense not to tell anyone about this so-called engagement?"

Sunny shook her head. "Paul only asked me this morning."

"I shall send him a note saying he is never to call on you, or speak to you, again. That will put an end to this idiocy." Augusta drummed her fingers on the elaborate desk as she thought. "Thornborough will be here in nine days. I shall give a ball in his honor a week later, and we can announce the betrothal then. The wedding should take place in October, I think. It will take that long to make suitable arrangements."

Knowing that she faced the fight of her life, Sunny wiped her damp palms on her skirt as she struggled for calm. "You must cable the duke and stop him from coming, Mother. Paul Curzon and I love each other, and I am going to marry him."

It was the first time she had ever defied her mother, and Augusta's jaw dropped in shock. Recovering quickly, she said in a low, furious voice, "You are a *Vangelder*, my girl, and I've devoted my life to training you to be worthy of the highest station. I will never permit you to throw yourself away on a worthless, fortune-hunting younger son!"

"Paul is no fortune hunter! He said that if you refused

permission, we could live on his income," Sunny said hotly. "And he isn't worthless! He's a British aristocrat, exactly what you wanted for me, and he has a great future in British politics. He was recently made a junior minister, and he says that with me by his side he'll soon be in the Cabinet."

"Your money would certainly help his career," Augusta said grimly, "but he'll have to find himself another heiress, because I will never give my consent."

"I don't need your consent!" Sunny said fiercely. "I'm of legal age and can marry whomever I wish. And I will!"

"How dare you speak to your mother this way!" Augusta grabbed Sunny's elbow, then marched her down the hall to her bedroom and shoved her inside. "If you think a humble life is so splendid, you can stay locked in here and live on bread and water until you change your mind!"

As the key turned in the lock, Sunny collapsed, shaking, on the bed. She had never dreamed how painful defiance could be. Yet she could not surrender, not when her whole life's happiness was at stake.

She must see Paul; he would know what to do.

The thought steadied her churning emotions, and she began to consider what to do. Her bedroom opened onto the roof of one of the porches, and her older brother Charlie had showed her how to climb to the ground. Her mother had never dreamed that her well-bred daughter would behave in such a hoydenish fashion.

Paul was staying at Windfall, which was only a mile away. Would he be there this evening? Yes, he'd mentioned that the Astors were giving a dinner party. She would wait until her mother retired, then escape and walk to Windfall.

With a veil over her face, no one would recognize her even if she was seen. She'd go to the servants' entrance and ask for the butler. He knew her, and she thought that for a suitable consideration he would summon Paul and let them have a few minutes of privacy.

Once they were together, everything would be all right.

❧

Sunny's plan went smoothly and by ten o'clock that evening she was pacing nervously around the Windfall servants' sitting room. She hoped Paul would be able to slip away quietly when the butler delivered her message. But what if the butler betrayed her to Mrs. Astor? Or if Mrs. Astor suspected that something was amiss and decided to investigate?

The door opened and she whirled around, ready to jump from her skin. With a wave of relief, she saw that it was Paul, devastatingly attractive in his evening dress. Coming toward her with concern on his face, he said, "Darling, you shouldn't risk your reputation like this. But it's wonderful to see you unexpectedly!"

He opened his arms and she went into them eagerly. She loved his height, which made her feel small and feminine. It was the first time they had real privacy, and his kiss far surpassed what they had shared before. Her resolve strengthened. She would never give up his love for the dubious pleasure of marrying a nondescript duke. Never!

Remembering the reason for her visit, she reluctantly ended the kiss. "Oh, Paul, something dreadful has happened!" she said miserably. "Today my mother told me that she has arranged for me to marry someone else. I told her about our betrothal, but she won't hear of it. She locked me in my room and swore I'd stay there on bread and water until I changed my mind."

"How dare she treat you in such a way!" Paul exclaimed. "I won't permit it!"

"I refused to agree to her wishes, of course, but it was so difficult. I...I think we should elope. Tonight."

"Right now?" he said, startled. "That's not what I want for you, darling. You deserve the grandest wedding of the century, not a furtive, hole-in-corner affair."

"What does that matter?" she said impatiently. "I'm trying to be strong, but my mother is...is not easy to resist."

"Who does she want you to marry?"

"The new Duke of Thornborough, Justin Aubrey. His brother, Gavin, just died, and Justin needs a rich wife."

Before she could say more, Paul said in a stunned voice, "The Duke of Thornborough! You would be one of the most influential women in England."

"And one of the unhappiest." Tears welled in her eyes, and she blinked them back angrily. "I need to be with you, Paul."

"We must reason this out." He stroked her back soothingly. "Your mother flatly refused to consider me as a suitor?"

"She said that it was unthinkable that I should marry a nobody." Sunny relaxed again, comforted by his touch. "Such nonsense! Titles mean nothing. What matters is being a gentleman, and no one is more gentlemanly than you."

After a long pause, Paul said gravely, "Sunny, I can't marry you against your mother's wishes. Though I knew that she would not be enthusiastic about my suit, I thought I would be able to persuade her. But to be Duchess of Thornborough! With that in prospect, she will never accept me."

A tendril of fear curled through Sunny. "It is not my

mother's place to choose my husband," she said sharply. "It's mine, and you are my choice. That's all that matters."

"If only it were that simple!" He sighed. "But it's not, my dear. You are not simply my own sweet love, but a national treasure, one of America's princesses. What kind of cad would I be to take advantage of your innocence to keep you from a glorious future?"

Sunny stared at him, thinking that this scene couldn't be real. Perhaps she had fallen off her bicycle and injured her head and everything that had happened since was only a bad dream. "You're saying you don't want to marry me?"

"Of course I do, but clearly that is impossible. If you marry me, you will become estranged from your family. I don't want to be the cause of that." He gazed lovingly into her eyes. "This won't be so bad, darling. In fact, one could see it as a piece of good fortune. With your influence to further my career, I'll be in the Cabinet in no time."

"Is that what matters most? Your career?" she said in a brittle voice.

"Of course not!" He pulled her close again. "The most important thing is our love, and your mother can't take that away from us. After you've given Thornborough an heir and a spare, we'll be free to love each other as we were meant to."

She went rigid, unable to believe what he was saying.

Feeling her withdrawal, he said tenderly, "I don't want to wait, either. If we're discreet, we can be together as soon as you're back from your honeymoon. Believe me, I would like nothing better! We'll have to be careful, of course. It wouldn't do to foist a bastard on Thornborough." He gave a wicked chuckle. "Though if the Gargoyle is unable to perform his duty, I'll be happy to help him. I look more like an Aubrey than he does."

"In other words, I make you a Cabinet minister, and my reward is adultery in the afternoon," she said numbly. "No, thank you, Mr. Curzon." Knowing that she would break down in tears if she stayed any longer, she headed for the door.

He followed her and caught her shoulders. "Don't look at it that way, darling! I promise you that this will turn out all right. We'll be able to enjoy the very cream of love, with none of the dreariness of daily living that kills romance."

He turned her around so that she was facing him. He was as heart-stoppingly handsome as ever, his golden hair glowing in the gaslight, his blue eyes limpid with sincerity.

She drew a shuddering breath. How could she have been such a fool?

His voice richly confident, he said, "Trust me, darling." He started to pull her toward him for another kiss.

She slapped him with all her strength. "You're right that this is a fortunate turn of events, because it's given me a chance to see what a swine you are!" she said, her voice shaking. "I hope never to see you again, though I don't suppose I'll be so lucky. Goodbye, Mr. Curzon, and good riddance."

As he gaped with shock, the imprint of her hand reddening on his face, she spun on her heel and bolted from the room. When she was outside the cottage, she took refuge in the shadowy lee of a huge hedge. There she fell to her knees, heart hammering and tears pouring down her face.

Ever since her childhood, she had dreamed of finding a man who would love her forever. She had wanted a marriage different from the carefully concealed hostility between her parents, or the bored civility common between many other fashionable couples. In Paul, she thought she had found the man she was seeking.

But she had been wrong, so wrong. Oh, he desired her body, and he lusted after her family's money and influence, but that wasn't love. She doubted that he knew what love was. Obviously she didn't know much about it, either. Perhaps the love she craved had never been more than a romantic girl's futile fantasy.

Blindly she stumbled to her feet and began the slow walk to The Tides. After Paul's betrayal, there was no reason to go anywhere else.

❧

The next morning, when a maid delivered a half loaf of freshly baked bread and a crystal pitcher of water on a tray decorated with a fresh rosebud, Sunny summoned her mother and said that she would accept the Duke of Thornborough's offer.

CHAPTER 3

*J*ustin found America a mixture of the sublime and the ridiculous. He liked the bustling energy of New York City and the cheerful directness of the average citizen. Yet in what was supposedly a nation of equals, he found people whose craven fawning over his title would have shamed a spaniel.

Newport society, which considered itself the crème de la crime of America, apparently wanted to out-Anglo the English when it came to formality and elaborate rules. Augusta Vangelder was in her element as she escorted him to an endless series of social events. She invariably referred to him as her "dear duke." He bore that stoically, along with all the other absurdities of the situation.

But the habits of the natives were of only minor interest; what mattered was Sunny Vangelder. He had hoped that she would greet him with the same sweet, unaffected good nature that she had shown at Swindon, perhaps even with eagerness.

Instead, she might have been a different person. The laughing girl had been replaced by a polished, brittle young woman who avoided speaking with him and never once met his gaze. Though he tried to revive the easy companionship they had so briefly shared, he had no success. Perhaps her stiffness was caused by her mother's rather repressive presence, but he had the uneasy feeling that there was a deeper cause.

His fifth morning in Newport, he happened to find Sunny reading in the library during a rare hour when they were at home. She didn't hear him enter, and her head remained bent over her book. The morning light made her hair glow like sun-struck honey, and the elegant purity of her profile caught at his heart.

It was time to make his formal offer of marriage. A flurry of images danced through his mind: him kneeling at her feet and eloquently swearing eternal devotion; Sunny opening her arms and giving him that wonderful smile that had made him feel as if he were the only man in the world; a kiss that would bring them together forever.

Instead, he cleared his throat to get her attention, then said, "Miss Vangelder—Sunny—there is something I would like to ask you. I'm sure you know what it is."

Perhaps she had known that he was there, for there was no surprise on her face when she lowered her book and looked up. "All of Newport knows," she said without inflection.

She wasn't going to make this easy for him. Wishing that he was skilled at spinning romantic words, he said haltingly, "Sunny, you have had my heart from the first moment I saw you at Swindon. There is no one else..."

She cut him off with an abrupt motion of her hand. "You needn't waste our time with pretty lies, Duke. We are here to strike a bargain. You need a fortune and a wife who knows what to do with a dinner setting that includes six forks. I need a husband who will lend luster to my mother's position in society, and who will confirm our fine American adage that anything can be bought. Please get on with the offer so I can accept and return to my book."

He rocked back on his heels, feeling as if he had been punched in the stomach. Wanting to pierce her contemptuous calm, he said with uncharacteristic bluntness, "We're talking about a marriage, not a business. The first duty of a nobleman's wife is to produce an heir, and knowledge of which fork to use will not help you there."

"I've heard that begetting children is a monstrously undignified business, but didn't the Queen tell her oldest daughter that a female needs only to lie there and think of England?" Sunny's lips twisted. "I should be able to manage that. Most women do."

Damning the consequences to Swindon, he said tightly, "There will be no offer, Miss Vangelder, for I will do neither of us a favor by marrying a woman who despises me."

Sunny caught her breath, and for the first time since he had arrived in Newport looked directly at him. He was shocked by the haunted misery in her aqua eyes.

After a moment she bent her neck and pressed her slim fingers to the center of her forehead. "I'm sorry, your grace. I didn't mean to imply that I despise you," she said quietly. "I recently... suffered a disappointment, and I'm afraid that my temper is badly out of sorts. Still, that does not excuse my insufferable rudeness. Please forgive me."

He guessed that only a broken heart would cause a well-mannered young lady to behave so brusquely. He had heard that Paul Curzon had been in Newport until the week before. Could Sunny have fallen in love with Curzon, who had as many mistresses as the Prince of Wales? Recalling how she had looked at the man when she was at Swindon, Justin knew it was all too likely.

The disappointment was crushing. When he had received Augusta Vangelder's invitation, he had assumed that she had obtained her daughter's agreement to the marriage. He should have known that he would never have been Sunny's choice. It was Augusta, after all, who was enthralled by the idea of a dukedom; Sunny was obviously unimpressed by the prospect.

In a voice of careful neutrality, he said, "You're forgiven, but even if you don't despise me, it's clear that this is not a match that you want." His throat closed, and it took an immense effort to add, "I don't want an unwilling bride, so if there is someone else whom you wish to marry, I shall withdraw."

She stared at her hands, which were locked tightly on her book. "There is no one I would prefer. I suppose that I must marry someone, and you'll make as good a husband as any."

He studied the delicate line of her profile, his resolve to do the right thing undermined by his yearning. Then she raised her head, her gaze searching. He had the feeling that it was the first time she had truly looked at him as an individual.

"Perhaps you would be better than most," she said after a charged silence. "At least you are honest about what you want."

It was a frail foundation for a lifetime commitment, but he could not bear to throw away this chance. "Very well," he said formally. "I would be very honored, and very pleased, if you would consent to become my wife."

"The honor is mine, your grace," she said with equal formality.

If this was a normal engagement, he would kiss his intended bride now, but Sunny's expression was unwelcoming, so he said only, "My name is Justin. It would please me if you used it."

She nodded. "Very well, Justin."

An awkward silence fell. Unhappily he wondered how achieving the fondest hope of his heart could feel so much like ashes. "Shall we go and inform your mother of our news?"

"You don't need me for that. I know that she is interested in an early wedding, perhaps October. You need only tell her what is convenient for you." Rubbing her temples, she set aside her book and got to her feet. "If you'll excuse me, I have a bit of a headache."

"I hope that you feel better soon."

"I'm sure I shall." Remembering that she had just agreed to give her life, her person and her fortune into this stranger's keeping, she attempted a smile.

It must not have been a very good attempt, because the duke's face remained grave. His thoughtful eyes were a clear, light gray, and were perhaps his best feature.

"I don't wish to seem inattentive," he said, "but my brother left his affairs in some disarray, and I must return to London the day after your mother's ball. I probably won't be able to return until a few days before the wedding."

"There is no need for romantic pretenses between us." She smiled, a little wryly, but with the first amusement she had felt since discovering Paul's true character. "It will be best if you aren't here, because there will be a truly vulgar amount of publicity. Our marriage will inevitably be deemed the Wedding of the Century, and there will be endless stories about you and me, your noble ancestors and my undistinguished ones, my trousseau, my flowers, my attendants and every other conceivable detail. And what the reporters can't find out, they will invent."

His dark brows arched. "You're right. It will be better if I am on the other side of the Atlantic." He opened the door for her.

When she walked in front of him, on impulse she laid her hand on his arm for a moment. "I shall do my best to be a duchess you will be proud of."

He inclined his head. "I'm sure you will succeed."

As she went upstairs to her room, she decided that he was rather attractive, in a subdued way. Granted, he wasn't much taller than she, but she was a tall woman. The quiet excellence of British tailoring showed his trim, muscular figure to advantage, and his craggy features had a certain distinction.

The words echoed in her mind, and as she entered her room and wearily lay on the bed, she realized that she had had similar thoughts when she first saw him at Swindon Palace.

That memory triggered others, and gradually fragments of that day came back to her. Lord Justin had been quiet but very gentlemanly, and knowledgeable about the gardens and estate. He had even showed signs of humor, of a very dry kind. It had been a pleasant interlude.

Yet he was still almost entirely a stranger, for she knew nothing of his mind or emotions. He didn't seem to be a man of deep feelings; it was his duty to marry well, so he was doing so, choosing a wife with his head rather than his heart.

Her eyes drifted shut. Perhaps this marriage would not be such a bad thing. She had heard that arranged marriages were happy about as often as love matches. She and the duke would treat each other with polite respect and not expect romance or deep passion. God willing, they would have children, and in them she might find the love she craved.

Certainly the duke had one great advantage: he could hardly have been more different from charming, articulate, false-hearted Paul Curzon.

﹩

*T*he maid Antoinette made a last adjustment to the train of Sunny's ball gown. "You look exquisite, mademoiselle. Monsieur le Duc will be most pleased."

Sunny turned and regarded herself in the mirror. Her cream-colored gown was spectacular, with sumptuous embroidery and a décolletage that set off her bare shoulders and arms perfectly. After her hair had been pinned up to expose the graceful length of her neck, fragile rosebuds had been woven into the soft curls. The only thing her appearance lacked was animation. "Thank you, Antoinette. You have surpassed yourself."

The maid permitted herself a smile of satisfaction as she withdrew. Sunny glanced at the clock and saw that she had a quarter of an hour to wait before making her grand entrance at the ball. The house hummed with excitement, for tonight Augusta's triumph would be announced. All of Newport society was here to fawn over Thornborough and cast envious glances at Sunny. There would also be sharp eyes watching to see how she and the duke—Justin— behaved with each other.

Antoinette, who was always well-informed, had passed on several disturbing rumors. It was said Sunny had at first refused to marry the duke because of his licentious habits, and that Augusta had beaten and starved her daughter into accepting him.

Even though there was a grain of truth in the story about her mother, Sunny found the gossip deeply distasteful. She must make a special effort to appear at ease with her mother and her fiancé. She looked in the mirror again and practiced her smile.

The door opened and a crisp English voice said, "How is my favorite goddaughter?"

"Aunt Katie!" Sunny spun around with genuine pleasure. "I had no idea that you were coming for the ball!"

"I told Augusta not to mention the possibility since I wasn't sure I would arrive in time." Laughing, Lady Westron held Sunny at arm's length when her goddaughter came to give her a hug. "Never crush a Worth evening gown, my dear! At least, not until the ball is over."

After a careful survey, she gave a nod of approval. "I'm madly envious. Even Worth can't make a short woman like me look as magnificent as you do tonight. The Newport cats will gnash their teeth with jealousy, and Thornborough will thank his stars for his good fortune."

Sunny's high spirits faded. "I believe he feels that we have made a fair bargain."

Katie cocked her head. "Are you unhappy about the match?"

Sunny shrugged and began drawing an elbow-length kid glove onto her right hand. "I'm sure that we'll rub along tolerably well."

Ignoring her own advice about crushing a Worth evening gown, Katie dropped into a chair with a flurry of satin petticoats. "I made inquiries about Thornborough when his solicitor first approached me about a possible match. He'll make you a better husband than most, Sunny.

He's respected by those who know him, and while he isn't a wit like his brother was and he's certainly not fashionable, he's no fool, nor is he the sort to humiliate you by flaunting his mistress."

Sunny stiffened. "Thornborough has a mistress?"

"Very likely. Most men do." Katie's lips curved ruefully. "There's much you need to learn about English husbands and English houses. Living in Britain is quite unlike being a visitor, you know."

Sunny relaxed when she found that her godmother had been talking in general rather than from particular knowledge. Though she knew that fashionable English society was very different from what she was used to, she disliked the idea of Thornborough with a mistress. Acutely.

She began the slow process of putting on her left glove. "Perhaps you had better educate me about what to expect."

"Be prepared for the fact that English great houses are cold." Katie shuddered. "Forget your delicate lace shawls! To survive winter in an English country house, your trousseau should include several wraps the size and weight of a horse blanket. You must have at least one decent set of furs, as well. The houses may be grand, but they're amazingly primitive. No central heating or gaslights, and no hot running water. And the bathrooms! A tin tub in front of the fire is the best you'll do in most houses."

Surprised and a little amused, Sunny said, "Surely Swindon Palace can't be that bad. It's said to be the grandest private home in Great Britain."

Katie sniffed, "A palace built almost two hundred years ago, and scarcely a pound wasted on modernization since then. But don't complain to Thornborough. English husbands, as a rule, are not solicitous in the way that American husbands are. Since the duke will not want to hear about your little grievances, you must learn to resolve matters on your own. I recommend that you take your own maid with you. That way you can count on at least one person in the household being on your side."

Sunny put a hand up. "If you say one sentence more, I will go downstairs and cancel my betrothal!" she said, not knowing whether to laugh or cry. "I'm beginning to wonder why any woman would want to marry an English lord, particularly if she isn't madly in love with him."

"I didn't mean to terrify you," Katie assured her. "I just want to make sure that you won't be disillusioned. Once a woman gets past the discomforts, she may have more freedom and influence than she would in America. Here, a woman rules her home, but nothing outside. An English lady can be part of her husband's life, or develop a life of her own, in a way most unusual in America."

Since frankness was the order of the day, Sunny asked, "Are you sorry you married Lord Westron?"

Katie hesitated a moment. "There are times when I would have said yes, but we've come to understand each other very well. He says that I've been invaluable to his political career, and through him, I've been able to bring a little American democracy to some hoary bits of British law." She smiled fondly. "And between us, we have produced three rather splendid children, even if I shouldn't say so myself."

Sunny sighed; it was all very confusing. She was glad when a knock sounded on her door. "Your mother says that it is time to come down, Miss Sarah," the butler intoned.

"Don't forget your fan. It's going to be very warm on the dance floor," Katie said briskly. "I'll be down after I've freshened up."

Sunny accepted the fan, then lifted her train and went

into the corridor. At the top of the sweeping staircase, she carefully spread the train, then slowly began descending the stairs, accompanied by the soft swish of heavy silk. She had been told that she walked with the proud grace of the Winged Victory. She ought to; as a child, she had been strapped into an iron back brace whenever she did her lessons. Perfect posture didn't come easily.

The hall below opened into the ballroom, and music and guests wafted through both. As she came into view, a hush fell and all eyes turned toward her. The cream of American society was evaluating the next Duchess of Thornborough.

When she was three-quarters of the way down, she saw that her fiancé was crossing the hall to the staircase. The stark black of formal evening wear suited him.

When she reached the bottom, he took her hand. Under his breath, he said, "You look even more beautiful than usual." Then he brushed a courtly, formal kiss on her kid-covered fingers.

She glanced at him uncertainly, not sure if he truly admired her or the compliment was mere formality. It was impossible to tell; he was the most inscrutable man she had ever met. Then he smiled at her and looked not merely presentable, but downright handsome. It was the first time she had seen him smile. He should do so more often.

Her mother joined them, beaming with possessive pride. "You look splendid, Sarah!"

A moment later they were surrounded by chattering, laughing people, particularly those who had not yet met the duke and who longed to rectify the omission. Sunny half expected her fiancé to retreat to a corner filled with men, but he bore up under the onslaught very well.

Though he spoke little, his grave courtesy soon won over even the most critical society matrons. She realized that she had underestimated him. Thornborough's avoidance of the fashionable life was obviously from choice rather than social ineptitude.

When she finally had a chance to look at her dance card, she saw that her fiancé had put himself down for two waltzes as well as the supper dance. That in itself was a declaration of their engagement, for no young lady would have more than two dances with one man unless intentions were serious.

When the orchestra struck up their first waltz, Thornborough excused himself from his admirers and came to collect her. She caught her train up so that she could dance, then took his hand and followed him onto the floor. "It will be a pleasure to waltz," she said. "I feel as if I've been talking nonstop for the last hour."

"I believe that you have been," he said as he drew her into position, a light hand on her waist "It must be fatiguing to be so popular. In the interests of allowing you to recover, I shan't require you to talk at all."

"But you are just as popular," she said teasingly. "Everyone in Newport wants to know you."

"It isn't me they're interested in, but the Duke of Thornborough. If I were a hairy ape from the Congo, I'd be equally in demand, as long as I was also a duke." He considered, then said with good-natured cynicism, "More so, I think. Apes are said to be quite entertaining."

Though Sunny chuckled, his remark made her understand better why he wanted her to call him Justin. Being transformed overnight from the Gargoyle to the much-courted Duke of Thornborough must have been enough to make anyone cynical.

It came as no surprise to learn that he danced well. She relaxed and let the voluptuous strains of music work their usual magic. The waltz was a very intimate dance, the closest a young woman was allowed to come to a man. Usually it was also an opportunity to talk with some privacy. The fact that she and Justin were both silent had the curious effect of making her disturbingly aware of his physical closeness, even though he kept a perfectly proper twelve inches between them.

Katie had been right about the heat of the ballroom; as they whirled across the floor, Sunny realized that a remarkable amount of warmth was being generated between their gloved hands. It didn't help that their eyes were almost level, for it increased the uncomfortable sense of closeness. She wished that she knew what was going on behind those enigmatic gray eyes.

A month before, she had waltzed like this with Paul Curzon and he had told her that his heart had driven him to follow her to America. The memory was jarring and she stumbled on a turn. If Justin hadn't quickly steadied her, she would have fallen.

His dark brows drew together. "Are you feeling faint? It's very warm. Perhaps we should go onto the porch for some air."

She managed a smile. "I'm fine, only a little dizzy. It's absurd that we can turn only one direction during a waltz. If we could spin the other way now and then, it would be much easier."

"Society thrives on absurdity," he observed. "Obscure rules are necessary so that outsiders can be identified and kept safely outside."

While she pondered his unexpected insight, the waltz ended and another partner came to claim her. The evening passed quickly. After the lavish supper was served, the engagement was formally announced. Augusta was in her element as even her most powerful social rivals acknowledged her triumph.

Sunny felt a pang as she accepted the good wishes of people she had known all her life. This was her last summer in Newport. Though she would visit in the future, it would not be the same; already her engagement to an Englishman was setting her apart.

The first phase of her life was ending—and she had no clear idea what the next phase would be like.

§

It was very late when the last of the guests left. As her official fiancé, Thornborough was allowed to escort Sunny to her room. When they reached her door, he said, "My train leaves rather early tomorrow, so I'll say goodbye now."

"I'm sorry that you'll have to travel without a proper night's sleep." Almost too tired to stand, she masked a yawn with her hand. "Have a safe and pleasant journey, Justin."

His gaze caught hers, and she couldn't look away. The air between them seemed to thicken. Gently he curved his hand around her head and drew her to him for a kiss.

Because she didn't love him she had been dreading this moment, yet again he surprised her. His lips were warm and firm. Pleasant. Undemanding.

He caressed her hair, disturbing the rosebuds, and scented petals drifted over her bare shoulder in a delicate sensual caress. She gave a little sigh, and his arms went around her.

The feel of his broad chest and his hand on the small of her back triggered a vivid memory of her last kiss, in Paul Curzon's embrace. All the anger and shame of that episode flooded back. She stiffened and took an involuntary step backward.

He released her instantly. Though his eyes had darkened, his voice was mild when he said, "Sleep well. I shall see you in October."

She opened her door, but instead of entering her room she paused and watched his compact, powerful figure stride down the hall to his own chamber. In spite of the warmth of the night, a shiver went down her spine. Her feelings about Justin were confused, but one thing was certain: it would be disastrous to continue to let the shadow of Paul Curzon come between her and her future husband. Yet she didn't know how to get rid of it.

CHAPTER 4

New York City
October 1885

*The **Wedding of the Century!***
Justin stared at the blaring headline in one of the newspapers that had just been delivered to his hotel room. It was a rude shock for a man who had disembarked in New York City only two hours earlier.

Below the headline were drawings of Sunny and himself. The likeness of him was not flattering. Were his brows really so heavy and threatening? Perhaps.

He smiled wryly as he skimmed the story, which was every bit as bad as Sunny had predicted. Apparently Americans had a maniacal interest in other people's private business. There was even a breathless description of the bride's garters, which were allegedly of gold lace with diamond-studded clasps. The item must have been invented, since he could not imagine Sunny discussing her gaiters with a reporter.

The thought of Sunny in her garters was so distracting that he swiftly flipped to the next newspaper. This one featured a cartoon of a couple getting married by a blindfolded minister. The tall, slim bride wore a martyred expression as she knelt beside a dissolute-looking groom who was half a head shorter.

The accompanying story implied rather strongly that the Duke of Thornborough was a corrupt specimen of European cad-hood who had come to the New World to coldly steal away the finest, freshest flower of American femininity. At the same time, there was an unmistakable undercurrent of pride that one of New York's own was to become a duchess. Apparently the natives couldn't decide whether they loathed or loved the trappings of the decadent Old World.

Disgusted, he tossed the papers aside and finished dressing for the dinner that Augusta Vangelder was giving in his honor. Afterward, the marriage settlements would be signed. Yet though that would make him a far wealthier man, what made his heart quicken was the fact that after three long months, he would see Sunny again. And not only see, but touch...

After his Newport visit they had written each other regularly, and he had enjoyed her whimsical anecdotes about the rigors of preparing for a wedding. If she had ever expressed any affection for him, he might have had the courage to tell her his own feelings, for it would be easier to write about love than to say the words out loud.

But her letters had been so impersonal that anyone could have read them. He had replied with equal detachment, writing about Swindon and acquainting her with what she would find there. He had debated telling her about some of the improvements he had ordered, but decided to keep them as a surprise.

He checked his watch and saw that the carriage the Vangelders were sending should be waiting outside the hotel. Brimming with suppressed excitement, he went downstairs.

As he crossed the lobby, a voice barked, "There he is!"

Half a dozen slovenly persons, obviously reporters, bolted across the marble floor and surrounded him. Refusing to be deterred, he kept walking through the babble of questions that came from all sides.

The loudest speaker, a fellow with a red checked vest, yelled, "What do you think of New York, Duke?"

Deciding it was better to say something innocuous rather than to ignore them entirely, Justin said, "A splendid city."

Another reporter asked, "Any of your family coming to the wedding, Duke?"

"Unfortunately that isn't possible."

"Is it true that Sunny has the largest dowry of any American girl to marry a British lord?"

The sound of her name on the man's lips made Justin glad that he wasn't carrying a cane, for he might have broken it across the oafs head. "You'll have to excuse me," he said, tight-lipped, "for I have an engagement."

"Are you going to visit Sunny now?" several chorused.

When Justin didn't answer, one of the men grabbed his arm. Clamping onto his temper, Justin looked the reporter in the eye and said in the freezing accents honed by ten generations of nobility, "I *beg* your pardon?"

The man hastily stepped back. "Sorry, sir! Duke. No offense meant."

Justin had almost reached the door when a skinny fellow jumped in front of him. "Are you in love with our Sunny, your dukeship, or are you only marrying her for the money?"

It had been a mistake to answer any questions at all, Justin realized; it only encouraged the creatures. "I realize that none of you are qualified to understand gentlemanly behavior," he said icily, "so you will have to take my word for it that a gentleman never discusses a lady, and particularly not in the public press. Kindly get out of my way."

The man said with a leer, "Just asking what the American public wants to know, Thorny."

"The American public can go hang," Justin snapped.

Before the reporters could commit any further impertinence, several members of the hotel staff belatedly came to Justin's rescue. They swept the journalists aside and escorted him outside with profuse apologies and promises that such persons would never be allowed in the hotel again.

In a voice clipped by fury, Justin told the manager, "I hope that is true, because if there is another episode like this I shall move to quieter quarters."

Temper simmering, he settled into the luxurious Vangelder carriage. The sooner this damned wedding was over and he could take his wife home, the better.

§

*S*unny was waiting in the Vangelder drawing room. She came forward with her hands outstretched, and if her smile wasn't quite as radiant as he would have liked, at least it was genuine.

"It's good to see you, Sunny." He caught her hands and studied her face hungrily. "You were right about the publicity surrounding the wedding. I'm afraid that I was just rather abrupt with some members of the press. Has it been hard on you?"

She made a face. "Though it's been dreadful, I'm well protected here. But everyone in the household has been offered bribes to describe my trousseau."

"Gold lace garters with diamond-studded clasps?"

"You saw that?" she said ruefully. "It's all so *vulgar*!"

She looked utterly charming. He was on the verge of kissing her when the door swung open. Justin looked up to see a tall, blond young man who had to be one of Sunny's older brothers.

"I'm Charlie Vangelder," the young man said cheerfully as he offered his hand. "Sorry not to meet you in Newport, Thornborough, but I was working on the railroad all summer. Have to learn how to run it when my uncle retires, you know."

So much for being alone with his intended bride. Suppressing a sigh, Justin shook hands with his future brother-in-law. A moment later, Augusta Vangelder swooped in, followed by a dozen more people, and it became clear that the "quiet family dinner" was an occasion for numberless Vangelders to meet their new relation by marriage.

The only break was the half hour when Justin met with the Vangelder attorneys to sign the settlement papers. His solicitor had bargained well; the minute that Justin married Sunny, he would come into possession of five million dollars worth of railway stock with a guaranteed minimum income of two hundred thousand dollars a year.

There would also be a capital sum of another million dollars that Justin would receive outright, plus a separate income for Sunny's personal use so that she would never have to be dependent on her husband's goodwill for pin money. As an incentive for Justin to try to keep his wife happy, the stock would revert to the Vangelder family trust if the marriage ended in divorce.

Gavin would have been amused to know that the value of the Thornborough title had risen so quickly. May Russell would have brought only half as much to her marriage.

Impassively Justin scrawled his name over and over, hating every minute of it. He wished that he could marry Sunny without taking a penny of her family money, but that was impossible. Without her wealth and his title, there would be no marriage.

As he signed the last paper, he wondered if Sunny would ever believe that he would have wanted her for his wife even if she had been a flower seller in Covent Garden.

&

*W*hen her daughter entered the breakfast parlor, Augusta said, "Good morning, Sarah." She took a dainty bite of buttered eggs. "There's a letter here for you from England."

Sunny tried unsuccessfully to suppress a yawn as she selected two muffins from the sideboard. The dinner party for Thornborough had gone on very late, and she had smiled at so many cousins that her jaw ached this morning.

She wished that she had had a few minutes alone with her future husband; she would have liked to tell him how much she had enjoyed his letters. She didn't know if it had been a deliberate effort on his part, but his descriptions of life at Swindon Palace had made her future seem less alien. His dry wit had even managed to make her smile.

She slit open the envelope that lay by her plate and scanned the contents. "It's from Lady Alexandra Aubrey,

Thornborough's youngest sister. A charming note welcoming me to the family."

Uncomfortably Sunny remembered that Katie had said the girl had been nicknamed the Gargoylette. Her lips compressed as she returned the note to the envelope. The girl might be small, shy and seventeen, but she was the only Aubrey to write her brother's bride, and Sunny looked forward to meeting her.

"Are you only going to have muffins for breakfast?" Augusta said with disapproval.

"After the dinner last night, it's all I have room for." Sunny broke and buttered one of the muffins, wondering why her mother had requested this private breakfast.

Expression determined, Augusta opened her mouth, then paused, as if changing her mind about what she meant to say. "Look at the morning paper. Thornborough was intemperate."

Obediently Sunny lifted the newspaper, then blinked at the screaming headline. ***Duke Tells American Public to Go Hang!***

"Oh, my," she said weakly. The story beneath claimed that Thornborough had bodily threatened several journalists, then bullied the hotel manager in a blatant attempt to infringe on the American public's constitutional right to a free press. "He mentioned yesterday that he'd been abrupt with some reporters, but surely this story is exaggerated."

"No doubt, but someone should explain to Thornborough that it's a mistake to pick fights with men who buy ink by the barrel." Augusta neatly finished the last of her meal. "A good thing that he was in England until now. Heaven knows what trouble he would have gotten into if he had been here longer."

Feeling oddly protective, Sunny said, "He's a very private man. He must find this vulgar publicity deeply offensive."

"Unfortunately, wealth and power always attract the interest of the masses."

Sunny poured herself coffee without comment. Her mother might say that public attention was unfortunate, but she would not have liked to be ignored.

Augusta began pleating her linen napkin into narrow folds. "You must be wondering why I wanted to talk to you this morning," she said with uncharacteristic constraint. "This will be difficult for both of us, but it's a mother's duty to explain to her daughter what her... her conjugal duties will be."

The muffin turned to sawdust in Sunny's mouth. Though she didn't want to discuss such a horribly embarrassing subject, there was no denying that information would be useful. Like all well-bred young ladies, her ignorance about marital intimacy was almost total.

Briskly Augusta explained the basics of male and female anatomy. Then, rather more slowly, she went on to describe exactly what a husband did to his wife.

Sunny choked on her coffee. "That's disgusting!" she said after she stopped coughing. She had heard whispered hints and giggles about the mysterious *something* that happened between men and women in the marriage bed, but surely it couldn't be what her mother was describing.

"It *is* disgusting," Augusta agreed, "as low and animal as the mating of hogs. It's also uncomfortable and sometimes painful. Perhaps someday scientific progress will find a better, more dignified way to make babies, but until then, women must suffer for the sins of Eve."

She took a piece of toast and began crumbling it between nervous fingers. "Naturally women of refinement are repulsed by the marital act. Unfortunately, men enjoy it. If they didn't, I suppose there would be no such thing as marriage. All a woman can do is lie there very quietly, without moving, so that the man will please himself quickly and leave her alone."

Lie there and think of England, in other words. Sunny's stomach turned. Had her tall, athletic father actually done such things to her delicate mother? Was this what Paul Curzon had wanted when he was kissing her? And dear God, must she really allow Thornborough such liberties? Her thighs squeezed together as her body rejected the thought of such an appalling violation.

Seeing her expression, Augusta said reassuringly, "A gentleman will not visit your bed more than once or twice a week. You also have the right to refuse your husband once you are with child, and for at least three months after you deliver." She glanced down at the pile of crumbs she had created. "Last night, after the settlements were signed, I took the duke aside and reminded him that you are gently bred, and that I would not permit him to misuse you."

"You spoke to Thornborough about this?" Sunny gasped, so humiliated that she wanted to crawl under the table and never come out "How did he reply?"

"He gave me the oddest look, but said that he understood my concern for your welfare, and assured me that he would be mindful of your innocence." Augusta gave a wintry smile. "It was very properly said. He is, after all, a gentleman."

Sunny's mind was a jumble of chaotic thoughts. The marriage bed sounded revolting—yet she had enjoyed Paul Curzon's kisses, and kissing was supposed to be a prelude to doing *it*. Surely the women who carried on flagrant affairs wouldn't do so if they found the whole business distasteful. Timidly she asked, "Do all women dislike the marital act?"

"I wish I could say that was so, but there is no denying that there are some women of our order who are a disgrace to their sex. Low-bred creatures who revel in their animal nature like barmaids! I know that you are not like that, but you will meet women who are." Leaning forward, Augusta said earnestly, "I cannot emphasize enough that it is fatal to seem to take pleasure in a gentleman's embrace. If you do, he will instantly lose all respect for you. A woman who acts like a prostitute will be treated like one. Always strive to maintain your dignity, Sarah. Ultimately it is all that a lady has."

With horror, Sunny remembered that when Paul had taken liberties, she had responded eagerly. Was that why he had made his degrading suggestion that she marry Thornborough, then have an affair with him? She still thought his behavior despicable—but perhaps she had brought it on by her wantonness. Paul had seen her acting like a slut, so he had treated her like one. It was exactly what her mother was warning her about.

Apparently a woman who gave in to her animal nature also risked unleashing a man's worst traits. That had been bad enough in the case of Paul Curzon, but Thornborough was going to be her husband! If he didn't respect her, the marriage would be hellish.

Feeling ill, Sunny said, "I shall remember all you have said and I will strive to behave in a manner that you would approve."

"I'm sure you will not disgrace your upbringing." Augusta bit her lip, her usual confidence gone. "Oh, Sarah, I'm going to miss you dreadfully. You'll be so far away."

Sunny resisted the temptation to point out that her

mother should have thought of that before accepting the proposal of a foreigner. "I'll miss you, too. You must visit us at Swindon soon."

Augusta shook her head. "Eventually, but not right away. I know that I'm a strong-minded woman, and I don't want to cause trouble between you and your husband. Marriage is a difficult business, and you and he must have time together with as little interference as possible."

At moments like this, Sunny loved her mother with painful intensity. It was true that Augusta was often domi-neering, yet her love for her children was very real. She was a woman of formidable energy. If she had a railroad or a bank to run, she might have been less absorbed in her daughter's life.

"I'll be fine," Sunny said with determined optimism. "Thornborough is a gentleman, and I am a lady. I'm sure that we can contrive a civilized marriage between us."

She wished that she was certain that was true.

CHAPTER 5

*T*ears flowing down her face, Sunny stood patiently while her maid laced up her white brocade bridal corset. Then Antoinette dropped the wedding gown over her head. It was magnificent, with foaming layers of Brussels lace and billows of white satin spangled with seed pearls and silver thread. Augusta had been so confident of her daughter's future triumph that she had ordered the gown from Worth when they visited Paris in March, before Sunny had ever set foot in London.

When the gown was fastened, Antoinette lifted the tulle veil and carefully draped it over the intricate coils of Sunny's hair. As the gauzy fabric floated down to her knees, the bride bleakly wondered if it was dense enough to conceal her tears.

Antoinette secured the veil with a coronet of orange blossoms, saying soothingly, "Don't fret, mademoiselle. Every girl is nervous on her wedding day. Monsieur le Due is a fine gentleman, and he will make you very happy."

Sunny's shoulders began shaking with the force of her sobs. Antoinette frowned and gave her a handkerchief, muttering, "Madame Vangelder should not have gone ahead to the church. A girl needs her mother at a time like this!"

As Sunny wept into the crumpled muslin square, a knock sounded at the door. Antoinette answered and returned with a large white flower box. "For you, mademoiselle."

"You can open it if you like," Sunny said drearily.

Less jaded than her mistress, Antoinette opened the package, disclosing an exquisite orchid bouquet nestled in layers of tissue paper. "There is a card for you, mademoiselle."

Sunny's puffy eyes widened when she read, "*These flowers are from the Swindon greenhouse. If they are suitable, perhaps you might wish to carry them. Fondly, Justin.*"

Oblivious to the fate of her five-yard-long train, Sunny dropped into a chair and wept even harder.

"Oh, mam'zelle!" Antoinette said helplessly. "What about the orchids makes you weep? They are very lovely."

"Yes, they are." Sunny made a desperate effort to collect herself. "I am ... touched by Thornborough's thoughtfulness in having them sent all the way from England."

Though it was not something she could say to her maid, she was even more moved by the fact that he was actually letting her choose whether or not to carry them. Every other detail of the wedding: the trousseau, the decorations, the extravagant reception, had been determined by her mother. Even the eight bridesmaids, including two Vangelder cousins, a Whitney, a Jay and an Astor, had been selected by Augusta for reasons of her own. Sunny had been swept along like a leaf in a torrent.

But Justin had given her a choice. Surely with such a considerate man, she could be happy. Unsteadily she said, "I must look like a fright. Please bring me some cold water and a facecloth." She glanced at the enormous bouquet Augusta had ordered. "You can set that aside. I will carry the orchids."

"But..." After the beginning of a protest, the maid nodded. "Yes, mademoiselle. An excellent choice."

As Antoinette went for the cold water, Sunny found herself wondering if the maid had ever endured the grotesquely undignified process of mating that Augusta had described. The thought almost sent her off in tears again.

For the last two days, at the most awkward moments, she had wondered the same thing about others: her brother Charlie, who was very fond of female company; the wife of the Anglican bishop who was going to perform the ceremony; Thornborough himself. Her morbid imaginings were turning her into a nervous wreck.

Antoinette returned with a basin of water and a cloth, then flipped the veil back over Sunny's head so that her face was bare. "You must hurry, mademoiselle, or you will be late."

As she sponged her stinging eyes with the cool, moist cloth, Sunny snapped, "They can all just *wait*!"

❦

The day became increasingly unreal. Fifth Avenue was lined on both sides with policemen assigned to prevent the thousands of spectators from breaking through. The wedding was to be at St. Thomas's Anglican church. Though the Vangelders didn't usually worship there, it was the only fashionable church with enough space for the seventy-voice choir Augusta had chosen.

Inside the church, huge arches of orange blossoms spanned the aisle, and banks of palms and chrysanthemums seemed to cover every vertical surface. Twenty-five excruciating minutes behind schedule, Sunny waited for her entrance, one icy hand clenched around her orchid bouquet and the other locked on her brother Charlie's arm. Though she couldn't see the guests clearly in the dim light, every pew was filled.

As the bridesmaids marched smartly down the aisle to the music of the sixty-piece orchestra, Charlie whispered, "Buck up, Sunny. Show them that an American girl is every bit the equal of any European princess."

The wedding march began, and Sunny started the long walk to the altar. If it hadn't been for her brother's firm support, the "American princess" might have fallen flat on her face.

With hysterical precision, she calculated that in the months since she had met Thornborough, they had seen each other for ten days, and been alone together for less than an hour. Why was she marrying a stranger? If it hadn't been for the five-yard train, she might have turned and bolted.

The dark figure of her fiancé waited impassively at the altar. Next to him was his best man, a pleasant fellow called Lord Ambridge, an old school friend of Justin's who was currently serving in the British Embassy in Washington.

As Sunny drew closer to her future husband, she saw that his expression was grim. Then she looked into his eyes and realized that he was as nervous as she. Her lateness must have made him wonder if she had changed her mind.

Dear God, how humiliating those long minutes of waiting must have been for him! As Charlie handed her over, she gave Thornborough an unsteady smile of apology.

His expression eased. He took her hand, and the

warmth of his clasp was the most real thing she had experienced all day.

They turned to face the bishop, and the ancient, familiar words transformed the stranger beside her into her husband.

❧

The wedding night was a disaster. Later Justin realized that it had been foolish of him to think it could have been otherwise, yet he had had the naive hope that once he and his bride were alone together, they would be able to relax. To become friends.

Instead, the "wedding breakfast" had proved to be a huge reception that seemed as if it would never end. By the time they reached their hotel suite, Sunny's face was gray with fatigue.

He wanted to hold her but restrained himself, for she looked as if she would shatter at a touch. They had a lifetime ahead of them; it would be foolish to rush matters now.

She mutely followed his suggestion that she relax with a long bath. Much later, after Sunny's maid had finished her ministrations and left for the night, he joined his wife in the spacious bedchamber. He expected to find her in the canopied bed, perhaps already asleep. Instead, she stood by the window, gazing out on the lights of New York.

He found her a far more interesting sight than the city. The glossy, honey-gold hair that flowed over her shoulders was even lovelier than he had imagined, and he longed to bury his face among the silken strands. Her white negligee frothed with lace and delicate embroidery and was so translucent that he could see the lithe shape of her body beneath. It must be another Worth creation; only a master could make a woman look simultaneously pure and provocative.

His *wife*. He was still awed by the miracle of it.

Justin had been introduced to the dark mysteries of passion when he was sixteen. Deciding it was time his young brother became a man, Gavin had taken Justin to a courtesan. With his usual careless kindness, Gavin had chosen the woman well. Lily was a warmhearted, earthily sensual Frenchwoman who had known exactly how to initiate a shy youth half her age.

Justin's shamed embarrassment had been gone by the end of his first afternoon with Lily. With her he had discovered not only passion, but kindness and mutual affection. He had visited her many times over the ensuing years. When her looks faded and she could no longer support herself as a courtesan, he had quietly bought her a cottage in the south of France so that she could retire in comfort. They still corresponded occasionally.

Because of Lily, he was now able to give his wife the gift of passion. Praying that desire would not make him clumsy, he went to join her by the window. Her delicate violet scent bewitched him, and his hands clenched with the effort of not touching her. Needing a safe, neutral topic, he said, "New York is lovely in a way quite distinct from London or Paris."

"I shall miss it," she whispered.

He glanced over and saw tears trembling in her eyes. "It must be hard to leave one's home," he said quietly, "but you can come back whenever you wish."

"Yes." She drew an unsteady breath. "Still, it hurts knowing that I am no longer an American. Though I understood that marrying a foreigner meant that I would lose my citizenship, I didn't expect to feel it so much."

"The law might say that you are now an Englishwoman, but it can't change what you are in your heart. America made you, and nothing can take that away."

After a long pause, she said in a low voice, "Thank you. I needed to be reminded of that."

Thinking the time was finally right, he put an arm around her waist. For the barest instant, she was pliantly yielding. Then she went rigid, like a small woodland creature holding still in the desperate hope that it would escape a predator's notice.

He turned her toward him and pulled her close, stroking her back in the hope that she would relax, but he was unsuccessful. Though she submitted without protest, her body remained as stiff as a marble statue.

Shyness or nerves were to be expected, but her reaction seemed extreme. He put his hands on her shoulders and held her away from him. "Sunny, are you afraid of me?"

"Not...not of you, really," she said, her eyes cast down.

It wasn't a heartening answer for an eager bridegroom. Patiently he said, "Then are you afraid of... marital intimacy?"

"It's more than that, Justin. I don't know quite how to explain." She pressed her hands to her temples for a moment, then looked into his eyes for the first time in days. "I was raised to be a wife. In the whole of my life, there was never any thought that I would ever be anything else." She swallowed hard. "Only now, when it's too late, does it occur to me that I don't really want to be married to anyone."

Though she claimed that he was not the problem, it was hard not to take her comments personally. Feeling a chill deep inside, he lowered his hands and said carefully, "What do you want me to do? Set you up in a separate establishment so that you never have to see me? File for an annulment on the grounds that your mother coerced you into marriage against your will?"

She looked shocked. "Of course not! I pledged my word today, and that can't be undone. I will do my best to be a good wife to you—but I don't know if I will succeed."

Some of the pain in his chest eased. As long as they were together, there was hope for building a loving marriage.

Though he had been counting the hours until they could be together, he said, "We needn't share a bed tonight, when you're so tired. It might be better to wait a few days until you're more at ease with me."

She hesitated, clearly tempted, before she shook her head. "I think it will be best to get it over with. Waiting will only give me more time to worry."

He wanted to make love to his wife, and she wanted to "get it over with," like a tooth extraction. Dear God, this was not what he had dreamed of! Yet perhaps she was right. Once she learned that intercourse was not as bad as she feared, she could relax and find pleasure in physical intimacy.

Yet he could not quite suppress the fear that his wife might never come to welcome his touch. He had been concerned ever since Augusta had ordered him to try to control his beastly animal nature. Obviously Augusta had loathed her own marital duties, and there was a strong possibility that she had passed her distaste on to her daughter.

His mouth tightened. Brooding would solve nothing. If his wife wanted the marriage consummated tonight, he would oblige. Partly because it might be the wisest course, but more because he wanted her with an intensity that was painful.

"Come then, my dear." He untied the ribbons of her negligee and pushed it from her shoulders so that she was clad only in a sheer silk nightgown that revealed more of her tantalizing curves than it concealed. He drew a shaky breath. It was how he had dreamed of her—and at the same time, it was utterly wrong, for she looked at him with the despairing eyes of a wounded doe.

She colored under his hungry gaze and glanced away. "Could you... would you turn the lamps out?"

Though he yearned to see her unclothed, he said, "As you wish."

As he put out the lights, she drew the curtains so that the windows were covered and the room became suffocatingly dark. Then she climbed into the bed with a faint creak of springs.

After removing his robe, he located the bed by touch and slid in beside her. He would have liked to take his nightshirt off, as well, but a man's naked body might upset her more, even in the dark and under blankets.

He drew her into his arms and kissed her with all the tenderness he had been yearning to lavish on her. Though she did not reject him, her mouth was locked shut and her whole frame was tense and unyielding. No amount of patient skill on his part could soften her. In fact, his feather kisses and gentle stroking seemed to make her more rigid. He felt as if he was trying to ravish a vestal virgin.

Despairing, he pushed himself up with one arm and said hoarsely, "This isn't right."

"Please, just do it," she said, an edge of hysteria in her voice.

His better nature surrendered, for despite his doubts,

his body was hotly ready, burning for completion. He reached for the lotion he had provided to ease this first union.

She gasped when he raised the hem of her gown, separated her legs and touched her intimately. He hoped that she might respond positively to his sensual application of the lotion, but there was no change. She simply endured, her limbs like iron, her breath coming in short, frightened gulps.

Though his blood pounded in his temples, he forced himself to go slowly when he moved to possess her. Her body resisted and he heard the scratch of her nails digging into the sheets, but she made no protest.

When the frail membrane sundered and he thrust deeply into her, she gave a sharp, pain-filled cry. He held still, waves of exquisite sensation sweeping through him, until her breathing was less ragged.

Then he began to move, and his control shattered instantly. He loved her and she was his, and he groaned with delirious pleasure as he thrust into her again and again.

His mindless abandon had the advantage of swiftness, for he could not have prolonged their coupling even if he tried. After the fiery culmination, he disengaged and lay down beside her, trembling with reaction. He yearned to hold her close and soothe her distress, but hesitated to touch her. "I'm sorry I hurt you," he panted. "It won't be this painful again."

"I'm all right, Justin," she said, voice shaking. "It...wasn't as bad as I expected."

It was a lie, but a gallant one. No longer able to restrain his impulse to cradle her in his arms, he reached out. If she would let him comfort her, something good would come of this night. But she rolled away into a tight little ball, and his searching fingers found only her taut spine.

The silence that descended was broken by the anguished sound of her muffled sobs. He lay still, drenched with self-loathing at the knowledge that he had found intoxicating pleasure in an act that had distressed her so profoundly.

After a long, long time, her tears faded and her breathing took on the slow rhythm of sleep. Quietly he slid from the bed and felt his way to the door that led to the sitting room, cracking his shin on a stool as he went.

A gas lamp burned in the sitting room, and he saw his haunted reflection in a mirror on the far wall. He turned away, unable to bear the sight of his own misery.

The suite was the most luxurious in the hotel, though not as richly furnished as the Vangelder houses. A porcelain bowl filled with potpourri sat on a side table. He sifted it through his fingers, and the air filled with a tangy fragrance.

He had reached for heaven and landed in hell. Their disastrous wedding night had not been the result of anything simple, like shyness on her part or ineptness on his part. It had been total rejection. The woman of his dreams couldn't bear his touch, and there seemed little chance that she would change in the future.

Vases of flowers were set all over the room. Some he had ordered, others were courtesy of the hotel, which was embarrassingly grateful to have the Duke and Duchess of Thornborough as guests. He pulled a white rose from an elegant cut-glass vase. It was just starting to open, at the perfect moment when promise met fulfillment.

Inevitably, he thought of Sunny when he had first seen her at Swindon. Exquisite, laughing, without flaw.

And now she lay weeping in the next room, her bright

gaiety gone. He supposed that part of the blame for that could be laid to a false lover, and part to Augusta, who loved her daughter with utter ruthlessness.

But most of the fault was his. By the simple act of wanting to marry her, he might have destroyed her blithe sweetness forever.

He began plucking out the satiny white petals, letting them drop one by one. She loved him, she loved him not, over and over, like a litany, as the scent of rose wafted around him.

The last petal drifted to the floor. She loved him not.

He lifted the vase and studied the artistry of the cut glass. Then, in one smooth, raging gesture, he hurled it across the room, where it shattered into a thousand pieces.

She loved him not.

CHAPTER 6

*J*ustin glanced out the train window at the rolling English landscape. "We'll reach Swindon station in about five minutes."

Sunny lifted her hat from the opposite seat and secured it to her coiled hair with a pearl-headed hat pin. Since they were traveling in the luxurious solitude of the Thornborough private car, she had had ample space for her possessions.

As she prepared for their arrival, she surreptitiously studied her husband. His expression was as impassive as always, even though he was bringing his bride home for the first time. Didn't he ever feel anything? In three weeks of marriage, he had never been anything but unfailingly polite. Civil. Kind. As remote as if he were on the opposite side of the earth.

Not that she should complain, for his calm detachment had made it possible to reach a modus vivendi very quickly. In public, she took his arm and smiled so that they presented a companionable picture to the world.

Naturally neither of them ever referred to what

happened in the silence of the night. Justin always ordered suites with two bedrooms so they could sleep separately. Every three or four days, with his gaze on the middle distance, he would ask if it was convenient for him to visit her.

She always gave her embarrassed assent, except for once when she had stammered that she was "indisposed." She would have died of mortification if he had asked what was wrong, but he had obviously understood. Five days passed before he asked again, and by then she was able to give him permission to come.

As he had promised, there had been no pain after the first occasion, and soon her fear had gone away. Dutifully she obeyed her mother's dictum and lay perfectly still while her husband did what husbands did. The marital act took only a few minutes, and he always left directly after.

Once or twice, she had felt his fingers brush through her hair before he climbed from the bed. She liked to think that it was a gesture of affection, though perhaps it was mere accident, a result of fumbling in the dark.

But her mother had been right; passive acceptance of her wifely role had won Justin's respect. Besides treating her with the utmost consideration, he also encouraged her to speak her opinions. That was certainly an unusual sign of respect, as well as a pleasure few wives had.

They discussed a wide variety of topics: British and American politics, art and music, architecture and history. Though Justin was never talkative, his observations were perceptive and he seemed to genuinely enjoy listening to her chatter. Best of all, the conversations were slowly building a rapport between them. It wasn't love—but perhaps someday it might be.

She prayed that that would happen, for living without love was a sad business.

Getting to her feet, she pulled on her sable-lined coat. Though it would warm her on the raw November day, that practical use was secondary. Before they left New York, her mother had emphasized that it was essential to wear her furs as a sign of wealth when she was first introduced to her new home and family. A good thing it wasn't August. Unable to see all of herself in the mirror, she asked, "Do I look all right?"

Her husband studied her gravely. "You look very lovely. Exactly as a duchess should, but seldom does."

The train squealed to a halt, and she glanced out to see a bunting-draped platform. "Good heavens!" she said blankly. "There are hundreds of people out there."

"I did warn you." He stood and walked to the carriage door. "It's probably the entire population of Swindon Minor and everyone for five miles around. The schools will have given a holiday so that the pupils can come and wave flags at you."

"It's different actually seeing them." Observing her husband's closed expression, she said, "You don't look very enthusiastic."

"Gavin was much better at this sort of thing." Perhaps that was true, but when Justin opened the door and stepped onto the platform, a roar of welcome went up. He gave a nod of acknowledgment, then turned to help Sunny step down. Another cheer went up, so she gave a friendly wave.

She met a blur of local dignities, all of whom gave speeches of welcome. Luckily she was good at smiling graciously, and the sables kept her from freezing in the chill, damp air.

The only part that stood out in her mind was the little

girl who was pushed forward, clutching a bouquet in her tiny hands. "Give the posies to the duchess, Ellie," her mother hissed.

Unclear on the theory, Ellie swept the bouquet around in circles. With a grin, Sunny intercepted it, then dropped a kiss on the child's soft brown curls. "Thank you, Ellie!"

Another cheer arose. Sunny blushed. Her gesture had not been calculated, but apparently kissing babies was good policy everywhere.

The mayor of the borough assisted her into the waiting carriage and Justin settled beside her. However, instead of starting for the palace, there was a delay while the horses were unhitched. A dozen men seized the shafts and began pulling the carriage up the village high street as the church bell began to ring clamorously.

Sunny gave her husband a doubtful glance. "This seems dreadfully feudal."

He lifted his hand in response to a group of exuberant uniformed schoolchildren. "This isn't really for you, or for me, either. It's a celebration of continuity. Of a life lived on this land for centuries. Swindon Palace belongs as much to the tenants as it does to the Aubreys."

She supposed he was right, and certainly the crowd seemed to be having a very jolly time. Nonetheless, her democratic American soul twitched a bit. Trying to look like a duchess, she smiled and waved for the slow two miles to Swindon Palace.

Another crowd waited in the courtyard. After the newlyweds had climbed the front steps, Justin turned and gave a short thank-you speech in a voice that carried easily to everyone present. Gavin might have had a talent for grand gestures, but the tenants had had more daily contact with Justin, and they seemed to heartily approve of him.

After one last wave, she went inside with her husband. The greetings weren't over yet, for a phalanx of Aubrey relations waited with a sea of servants behind them.

As she steeled herself for more introductions and smiles, two huge wolfhounds galloped toward the door, nails scrabbling on the marble floor. The sight of the enormous dogs charging full speed at her made Sunny give a small squeak of alarm.

Before the beasts could overrun them, Justin made a quick hand gesture and commanded, "Sit!"

Instantly the wolfhounds dropped to their haunches, though they wriggled frantically for attention. Justin stroked the sleek aristocratic heads, careful not to neglect either. "These were Gavin's dogs. They miss him dreadfully."

To Sunny, it looked as if the wolfhounds were perfectly satisfied with the new duke. It took a moment to realize that Justin's comment was an oblique admission of his own grief.

She was ashamed of the fact that she had not really considered how profoundly he must feel his brother's death. Though the two men had been very different, the first time she had seen them they had been standing side by side. They must have been close, or Justin would not have chosen to manage the family property when he could have done many other things.

While she was wondering if she should say something to him, the relatives descended. First in consequence was the dowager duchess, Justin's mother, who wore mourning black for Gavin. Her forceful expression reminded Sunny of her own mother, though Augusta was far more elegant.

After a fierce scrutiny of the colonial upstart, the dowager said, "You look healthy, girl. Are you pregnant yet?"

As Sunny flushed scarlet, Justin put a protective arm around her waist. "It's a little early to think about that since we've been married less than a month, Mother," he said calmly. "Sunny, I believe you already know my older sisters, Blanche and Charlotte, and their husbands, Lord Alton and Lord Urford."

Sunny had met all four in London during the season. The sisters were in the same mold as Gavin: tall, blond, handsome Aubreys whose self-absorption was tempered by underlying good nature. They examined Sunny's furs with frank envy, but their greetings were friendly. After all, it was her money that would keep up the family home.

Next in line was Lady Alexandra, the Gargoylette. She hung back until Justin pulled her into a hug. It was the most affectionate Sunny had ever seen him. "I don't believe you've met my little sister, Alexandra."

He accompanied his introduction with a speaking look at his wife. Sunny guessed that if she was dismissive or abrupt, he would not easily forgive her.

Alexandra stammered a greeting, too bashful to meet her new sister-in-law's eyes. Dark and inches shorter than the older girls, she looked very like Justin. There was nothing wrong with her appearance except that her mother dressed her very badly.

Following her instinct, Sunny also hugged her smallest sister-in-law. "Thank you so much for your letter!" she said warmly. "It was good to know that I would find a friend here."

Alexandra looked up shyly. Her gray eyes were also like Justin's, but where he was reserved, she was vulnerable. "I'm glad you're here," she said simply. "I saw you when you came to the garden fete last spring, and thought you were the loveliest creature in the world."

A little embarrassed at such frank adoration, Sunny said lightly, "It's amazing what a good dressmaker can do."

Then it was onward to sundry Aubrey cousins and shirt-tail relations. After that, the butler and housekeeper, two *very* superior persons, welcomed her as their new mistress and presented her with a silver bowl as a wedding gift from the household.

While Sunny wondered how much the poor servants had been forced to contribute, she was paraded past ranks of maids and footmen as if she were a general reviewing troops. Finally it was time to go upstairs to prepare for dinner.

Justin escorted her to her new rooms. The duchess's private suite was rather appallingly magnificent. Eyeing the massive, velvet-hung four-poster bed, Sunny asked, "Did Queen Elizabeth sleep there?"

"No, but Queen Anne did." The corner of Justin's mouth quirked up. "I know it's overpowering, but I didn't order any changes because I thought you'd prefer to make them yourself."

Sunny thoughtfully regarded a tapestry of a stag being torn apart by a pack of dogs. "I don't care if it is priceless, that tapestry will have to go. But I can bear it for now. How long do I have until dinner?"

"Only half an hour, I'm afraid. There's more to be seen, but it can wait." He gestured to a door in the middle of one wall. "That goes directly to my bedchamber. Don't hesitate to ask if there's anything you need."

"I'm too confused to know what I need, but thank you." Sunny took off her hat and massaged her throbbing temples. "Should you and I go down together for dinner?"

"Definitely," he replied. "Without a guide to the dining room, you'd probably get lost for a week."

After Justin left, Antoinette emerged from the dressing room. "While everyone was welcoming you, madam, I had time to unpack your clothing. What do you wish to wear tonight? Surely something grand to impress the relations."

"The butter-cream duchesse satin, I think." Sunny considered. "I suppose I should also wear the pearl and diamond dog collar, even though it chafes my neck."

The maid nodded with approval. "No one will be your equal!"

After Antoinette disappeared to prepare the gown, Sunny sank into a brocade-covered chair. It was hideously uncomfortable, which was fortunate, because otherwise she might fall asleep.

It was pleasant to have a few minutes alone. In spite of the wretched chair, she was dozing when Antoinette bustled back. "Madam, I have found something wonderful! You must come see." Sunny doubted that anything was worth such enthusiasm, but she obediently rose and followed her maid into the dressing room. Two doors were set into the opposite wall. Antoinette dramatically threw open the right-hand one. "Voila!"

Sunny's eyes widened. It was a bathroom that would have impressed even Augusta Vangelder. The mahogany-encased tub was enormous, and the floor and walls had been covered in bright, exquisitely glazed Spanish tiles. "You're right! It's the most gorgeous bathroom I've ever seen."

"And the next room over—" the maid pointed "—is a most splendid water closet. The chambermaid who brought in the towels said that Monsieur le Due had all this done for you after the betrothal was announced."

Amused and touched, Sunny stroked a gleaming tile. It appeared that she would not have to suffer the country house horrors that Katie Westron had warned her about. "Perhaps later tonight I will take advantage of this."

Wanting to give credit where credit was due, she went to her bedchamber and opened the connecting door to the duke's suite. "Justin, I have found the bathing room and—"

In the middle of the sentence, her gaze found her husband and she stopped dead. She had caught him in the middle of changing his clothing. He had just taken off his shirt, and she blushed scarlet at the sight of his bare chest.

Though his brows rose, he did not seem at all discomposed. "Having seen the wonders of the American plumbing, I knew that you would find Swindon rather primitive," he said. "Making some improvements seemed like a more useful wedding gift than giving you jewels."

Though she tried to look only into his eyes, her gaze drifted lower. He was broad-shouldered and powerfully muscled, which was why he didn't have a fashionable look of weedy elegance. She wondered how the dark hair on his chest would feel to her touch.

Blushing again, she said hastily, "Your idea was inspired. I've always loved long baths, and I'd resigned myself to having to make do with a tin tub in front of the fire."

"Speaking of fires, I decided that it was also time to install central heating." Justin casually pulled on a fresh shirt, though he didn't bother to button it. "It will be a long time until the whole building is completed, but I had the workers take care of this wing first, so you would be comfortable. I know that Americans like their houses warm."

Only then did she notice that the rooms were much warmer than she should have expected. "Thank you, Justin! I think you must be the most considerate husband on earth." She crossed the room to her husband's side and gave him a swift kiss.

It was the first time she had ever done such a thing, and she wondered belatedly if he would think her too forward. But he didn't seem to mind. His lips moved slowly under hers, and he raised his hand and massaged the back of her neck.

He had a tangy masculine scent that was distinctly his own. Succumbing to temptation, she let her fingers brush his bare chest as if by accident. The hair was softer than she had expected, but she felt unnerved when his warm flesh tensed at her touch. Hastily she lowered her hand.

But the kiss continued, and she found that she was in no hurry to end it. Very gently, his tongue stroked her lips. It was a new sensation, but pleasant. Very pleasant....

The clamor of a bell reverberated brassily through the corridors. Both of them jumped as if they had been caught stealing from the church poor box.

After he had caught his breath, Justin said, "The predinner bell. We must be downstairs in ten minutes."

"I barely have time to dress." Embarrassed at how she had lost track of time, Sunny bolted to her own room. As soon as the connecting door was closed, Antoinette started unfastening her traveling dress so that the duchesse satin could be donned.

Yet as her maid swiftly transformed her, Sunny's mind kept returning to the kiss, and her fingertips tingled with the memory of the feel of her husband's bare body.

&

*D*inner was another strain. Sunny sat at the opposite end of the table from her husband, so far away that she could barely see him.

Before the first course had been removed, it was obvious that the dowager duchess was a tyrant, with all the tact of a charging bull. She made a string of remarks extolling Gavin's noble spirit and aristocratic style, interspersed with edged comments about the deficiencies of "poor dear Justin."

Charlotte tried to divert the conversation with a cheerful promise to send Sunny a copy of the table of precedence so that she would never commit the cardinal crime of seating people in the wrong order. That inspired the dowager to say, "There are about two hundred families whose history and relationships you must understand, Sarah. Has Justin properly explained all the branches of the Aubreys and of my own family, the Sturfords?"

"Not yet, Duchess," Sunny said politely.

"Very remiss of him. Since he wasn't raised to be a duke, he hasn't a proper sense of what is due his station." The dowager sniffed. "So sad to see poor dear Justin in his brother's place. Such a comedown for the family. You must be quick about having a child, Sarah, and make sure it's a boy."

Sunny was tempted to sling the nearest platter of veal collops at her mother-in-law, but it seemed too soon to get into a pitched battle. A quick glance at her husband showed that he had either not heard his mother, or he chose to ignore her. Clearly Alexandra had heard, for she was staring at her plate, her face flushed.

Carefully Sunny said, "The eighth duke's death was a great tragedy. You all have my sympathies on your loss."

The dowager sighed. "Gavin should have betrothed himself to you, not that Russell woman. If he had, he might be alive now, in his proper place."

Sunny had heard enough gossip to know that the fatal problem had not been Gavin's fiancée, but his inability to keep his hands off other women, even when on the way to his own wedding. Hoping to end this line of discussion, she said piously, "It is not for us to question the ways of heaven."

"A very proper sentiment," the dowager said. "You have pretty manners. One would scarcely know you for an American."

Did the woman suppose that she was giving a compliment? Once more Sunny bit her tongue.

Yet in spite of her good intentions, she was not to get through the evening peacefully. The gauntlet was thrown down at the end of the lengthy meal, when it was time for the ladies to withdraw and leave the gentlemen to their port. Sunny was about to give the signal when the dowager grandly rose to her feet and beat Sunny to it.

As three women followed the dowager's lead, Sunny's blood went cold. This was a direct challenge to her authority as the new mistress of the household. If she didn't assert herself immediately, her mother-in-law would walk all over her.

The other guests hesitated, glancing between the new duchess and the old. Sunny wanted to whimper that she was too *tired* for this, but she supposed that crises never happened at convenient times. Though her hands clenched below the table, her voice was even when she asked, "Are you feeling unwell, Duchess?"

"I am in splendid health," her mother-in-law said haughtily. "Where did you get the foolish idea that I might be ailing?"

"I can think of no other reason for you leaving prematurely," Sunny said with the note of gentle implacability that she had often heard in her mother's voice.

For a moment the issue wavered in the balance. Then, one by one, the female guests who had gotten to their feet sank back into their seats with apologetic glances at Sunny. Knowing that she had lost, the dowager returned to the table, her expression stiff with mortification.

As she waited for a decent interval to pass before leading the ladies from the table, Sunny drew in a shaky breath. She had won the first battle, but she knew there would be others.

❦

The evening ended when the first clock struck eleven. Accompanied by the bonging of numerous other clocks, Justin escorted his wife upstairs. When they reached the door of her room, he said, "I'm sorry that it's been such a long day, but everyone was anxious to meet you."

She smiled wearily. "I'll be fine after a night's sleep."

"You were a great success with everyone." After a moment of hesitation, he added, "I'm sorry my mother was so... abrupt. Gavin was her favorite, and she took his death very badly."

"You miss him, too, but it hasn't made you rude." She bit her lip. "I'm sorry, I didn't mean to sound impertinent."

"My mother is a forceful woman, and I don't expect that you'll always agree. Blanche and Charlotte used to have terrible battles with her. Just remember that you are my wife, and the mistress of Swindon."

"I shall attempt to be tactful while establishing myself." She made a rueful face. "But I warn you, I have trouble countenancing unkind remarks about other people."

That sensitivity to others was one of the things he liked best about her. A volatile mix of tenderness and desire moved through him, and he struggled against his yearning to draw her into his arms and soothe her fatigue away.

He might have done so if he hadn't been aware that the desire to comfort would be followed by an even more over-whelming desire to remove her clothing, garment by garment, and make slow, passionate love to her. With the lamps lit, not in the dark.

Innocently she turned her back to him and said, "Could you unfasten my dog collar? It's miserably uncomfortable."

The heavy collar had at least fifteen rows of pearls. As he undid the catch and lifted the necklace away, he saw that the diamond clasp had rubbed her tender skin raw. He frowned. "I don't like seeing you wearing something that hurts you."

She sighed. "Virtually every item a fashionable woman wears is designed to hurt."

He leaned forward and very gently kissed the raw spot on her nape. "Perhaps you should be less stylish."

She tensed, as she did whenever he touched her in a sensual way. "A duchess is supposed to be fashionable. I would be much criticized if I didn't do you credit." Eyes downcast, she turned and took the jeweled collar, then slipped into her room.

He felt the familiar ache as he watched her disappear. Who was it who said that if a man wanted to be truly lonely, he should take a wife? It was true, for he didn't recall feeling lonely before he married.

But now that he had a wife, his life echoed with loneliness. The simple fact was that he wanted more of her. He wanted to hold her in his arms all night while they slept. He wanted her to sigh with pleasure when he made love to her. He wanted to pour tea for her at the breakfast table. He wanted to be with her day and night.

He drew a deep breath, then entered his room and began undressing. He had hoped that with time she might come to enjoy intimacy more, but every time he came to her bed, she became rigid. Though she never complained, or spoke at all, for that matter, it was clear that she could scarcely endure his embraces.

Yet she didn't seem to dislike him in other ways. She talked easily and was willing to share her opinions. And she had given him that shy kiss earlier. In her innocence, she had not understood that she set the blood burning through his veins. But even going to her bed would not have quenched the fire, for he had found that quick, furtive coupling was more frustrating than if he had never touched her.

As he slid into his bed, he realized how foolish it was of him to object to a necklace that chafed her neck when his conjugal demands disturbed her far more. He despised himself for taking that which was not willingly given, yet he was not strong enough to prevent himself from going to her again and again. His twice weekly visits were his compromise between guilt and lust.

He stared blindly into the darkness, wondering if he would be able to sleep.

If you would be lonely, take a wife.

CHAPTER 7

Swindon
February 1886

*S*unny abandoned her letter writing and moved to her sitting room window, staring out at the gray landscape. In the distance was a pond where long ago a footman had drowned himself in a fit of melancholy. As the dreary winter months dragged by, she had come to feel a great deal of sympathy for the poor fellow.

The loudest sound was the ticking of the mantel clock. Swindon was full of clocks, all counting out the endless hours.

She glanced at the dog curled in one of the velvet-covered chairs. "Daisy, how many of the women who envied my glamorous marriage would believe how tedious it is to winter on an English country estate?"

Daisy's floppy-eared head popped up and she gave a sympathetic whimper. Unlike the beautiful but brainless wolfhounds, Daisy, a small black-and-tan dog of indeterminate parentage, was smart as a whip. Sunny liked to think that the dog understood human speech. Certainly she was a good listener.

Her gaze went back to the dismal afternoon. Custom decreed that a bride should live quietly for a time after her wedding, and at Swindon, that was very quietly indeed. Apart from the newlyweds, Alexandra and the dowager were the only inhabitants of the vast palace. There were servants, of course, but the line between upstairs and downstairs was never crossed.

The best part of the daily routine was a morning ride with Justin. Sunny never missed a day, no matter how vile the weather, for she enjoyed spending time with her husband, though she couldn't define the reason. He was simply... comfortable. She only wished that she understood him better. He was like an iceberg, with most of his personality hidden from view.

After their ride, she usually didn't see him again until dinner, for estate work kept him busy. Occasionally he went to London for several days to attend to business. He was gone now, which made the hours seem even longer.

The high point of country social life was making brief calls on neighbors, then receiving calls in turn. Though most of the people Sunny met were pleasant, they lived lives as narrow and caste-ridden as Hindus.

Luckily even the most conventional families usually harbored one or two splendid eccentrics in the great British tradition. There was the Trask uncle who wore only purple clothing, for example, and the Howard maiden aunt who had taught her parrot all the basic social responses so that the bird could speak for her. Such characters figured prominently in Sunny's letters home, since little else in her life was amusing.

A knock sounded at the door. After Sunny called permission to enter, her sister-in-law came into the sitting room. "A telegram arrived for you, Sunny, so I said I'd bring it up." Alexandra handed it over, then bent to scratch Daisy's ears.

Sunny opened the envelope and scanned the message. "Justin finished his business early and will be home for dinner tonight."

"That's nice. It's so quiet when he's away."

"Two months from now, after you've been presented to society and are attending ten parties a day, you'll yearn for the quiet of the country."

Alexandra made a face. "I can't say that I'm looking forward to being a wallflower at ten different places a day."

"You're going to be a great success," Sunny said firmly. "It's remarkable what good clothing can do for one's confidence. After Worth has outfitted you, you won't recognize yourself."

Unconvinced, Alexandra returned to petting Daisy. Though young in many ways, the girl was surprisingly mature in others. She was also well-read and eager to learn about the world. The two young women had become good friends.

Deciding that she needed some fresh air, Sunny said, "I think I'll take a walk before I bathe and change. Would you like to join me?"

"Not today, thank you. I have a book I want to finish." Alexandra grinned, for at the word "walk," Daisy jumped to the floor and began skipping hopefully around her mistress. "But someone else wants to go. I'll see you at dinner."

After Alexandra left, Sunny donned a coat—not the

sables, but a practical mackintosh—and a pair of boots, then went down and out into the damp afternoon, Daisy frisking beside her.

Once they were away from the house, Sunny asked, "Would you like to play fetch?" Foolish question; Daisy was already racing forward looking for a stick.

Sunny had found Daisy on a morning ride not long after her arrival at Swindon. The half-grown mongrel had been desperately trying to stay afloat in the overflowing stream where someone had probably pitched her to drown.

Driven frantic by the agonized yelps, Sunny had been on the verge of plunging into the water when Justin had snapped an order for her to stay on the bank. Before she could argue, he'd dismounted and gone after the young dog himself.

When Sunny saw her husband fighting the force of the current, she realized that he was risking his life for her whim. There had been one ghastly moment when it seemed the water would sweep him away. As her heart stood still, Justin managed to gain his footing, then catch hold of the struggling dog.

After sloshing out of the stream, he had handed her the shivering scrap of canine with the straight-faced remark that it was quite an appealing creature as long as one didn't have any snobbish preconceptions about lineage. The sodden pup had won Sunny's heart with one lap of a rough tongue. She'd had almost wept with gratitude, for here was a creature who loved her and whom she could love in return.

Naturally the dowager duchess had disliked having such an ill-bred beast at Swindon, but she couldn't order the dog out of the house when Justin approved. The dowager had resorted to mumbled comments that it was natural for

Sunny to want a mongrel, since Americans were a mongrel race. Sunny ignored such remarks; she'd become very good at that.

As always, Daisy's desire to play fetch exceeded Sunny's stamina. Abandoning the game, they strolled to the little Greek temple, then wandered toward the house while Sunny thought of changes she would make in the grounds. A pity that nothing could be done at this time of year, for gardening would cheer her up.

In an attempt to stave off self-pity, she said, "I'm really very fortunate, Daisy. Most of Katie Westron's dire warnings haven't come true. Justin is the most considerate of husbands, and he is making the house very comfortable." She glanced toward the palace, where men labored on the vast roof despite the weather. "My ceiling hasn't leaked since before Christmas."

She made a wry face. "Of course, it might be considered a bit strange that I talk more to a dog than to my husband."

One of Katie's warnings haunted her—the possibility that Justin might have a mistress. Could that be the real reason for his business trips? She loathed the thought that her husband might be doing those intimate, dark-of-the-night things to another woman. She tried not to think of it.

The dull afternoon had darkened to twilight, so she summoned Daisy and headed toward the house. If the best part of the day was riding with Justin, the worst was dining with the dowager duchess. Familiarity had not improved her opinion of her mother-in-law. Most of the dowager's cutting remarks were directed at Justin, but she also made edged comments about Alexandra's lack of looks and dim marital prospects. She usually spared Sunny, rightly suspecting that her daughter-in-law might strike back.

Sunny wondered how long it would be before she

disgraced herself by losing her temper. Every meal brought the breaking point closer. She wished that Justin would tell his mother to hold her tongue, but he was too courteous, or detached, to take action.

When she got to the house, she found that her husband was in the entry hall taking off his wet coat. She thought his expression lightened when he saw her, but she wasn't sure; it was always hard to tell with Justin.

"Hello." She smiled as she took off her mackintosh. "Did you have a good trip to London?"

As the butler took away the coats, Justin gave Sunny a light kiss on the cheek, then rumpled Daisy's ears. He was rather more affectionate with the dog. "Yes, but I'm glad to be home."

He fell into step beside her and they started up the main stairs. The thought of a possible mistress passed through Sunny's mind again. Though she knew that it was better not to probe, she found herself saying, "What are all these trips about, or wouldn't I be able to understand the answer?"

"The Thornborough income has traditionally come from the land, but agriculture is a chancy business," he explained as they reached the top of the stairs. "I'm making more diverse investments so that future dukes won't have to marry for money."

She stopped in mid-stride, feeling as if he had slapped her. When she caught her breath, she said icily, "God forbid that another Aubrey should have to stoop to marrying a mongrel American heiress."

He spun around, his expression startled and distressed. "Sunny, no! I'm sorry, I didn't mean that the way it sounded."

Her brows arched. "Oh? I can't imagine any meaning other than the obvious one."

When she turned and headed toward the door of her suite, he caught her arm and said intensely, "You would have been my choice even if you weren't an heiress."

Her mouth twisted. "Prettily said, but you needn't perjure yourself, Justin. We both know this marriage wouldn't have been made without my money and your title. If you invest my money wisely, perhaps our son, if we have one, will be able to marry where he chooses. I certainly hope so."

Justin's hand fell away and Sunny escaped into her sitting room, Daisy at her heels. When she was alone, she sank wretchedly into a chair. She had been better off not knowing what Justin really felt.

Before she had wondered if he had a mistress; now, sickeningly, she wondered if he had a woman who was not only his mistress, but his beloved. There had been a raw emotion in his voice that made her think, for the first time, that he was capable of loving deeply. Had he been forced to forsake the woman he loved so that he could maintain Swindon?

Sensing distress, Daisy whimpered and pushed her cool nose into Sunny's hand. Mechanically she stroked the dog's silky ears. What a wretched world they lived in! But even if Justin loved another woman, he was her husband and she must make the best of this marriage. Someday, if she was a very good wife, perhaps he would love her, at least a little.

She desperately hoped so, for there was a hole in the center of her life that the frivolity of the Season would never fill.

*S*unny's depression was not improved by the discovery that the dowager duchess was in an unusually caustic mood. Throughout an interminable dinner, she made acid remarks about the neighbors, the government and most of all her son.

As fruit and cheese were served, she said, "A pity that Justin hasn't the Aubrey height and coloring. Gavin was a much more handsome man, just as Blanche and Charlotte are far prettier than Alexandra."

Suppressing her irritation, Sunny said coolly, "I've studied the portraits and the first duke, John Aubrey, was dark and of medium build. Justin and Alexandra resemble him much more than your other children do."

The dowager sniffed. "The first duke was a notable general, but though it pains me to admit it, he was a very low sort of man in other ways. A pity that the peasant strain hasn't yet been bred out of the family." She gave an elaborate sigh. "Such a tragedy that Justin did not die instead of Gavin."

Sunny gasped, stunned. How *dare* that woman say she wished Justin had died in his brother's place! Justin was worth a dozen charming, worthless wastrels like Gavin. She glanced at her husband and saw that he was carefully peeling an apple, as if his mother hadn't spoken, but there was a painful bleakness in his eyes.

If he wouldn't speak, she would. Laying her fork beside her plate, she said flatly, "You must not speak so about Justin, Duchess."

"You forget who I am, madam." The dowager's eyes gleamed with pleasure at the prospect of a battle. "As the mother who suffered agonies to bear him, I can say what I wish."

"And you forget who I am," Sunny said with deadly precision. "The mistress of Swindon Palace. And I will no longer tolerate such vile, ill-natured remarks."

The dowager gasped, her jaw dropping open. "How dare you!"

Not backing down an inch, Sunny retorted, "I dare because it is a hostess's duty to maintain decorum at her table, and there has been a sad lack of that at Swindon."

The dowager swept furiously to her feet. "I will not stay here to be insulted by an impertinent American!"

Deliberately misinterpreting her mother-in-law's words, Sunny said, "As you wish, Duchess. I can certainly understand why you prefer to have your own establishment. If I were to be widowed, I would feel the same way. The Dower House is a very charming residence, isn't it?"

The dowager's jaw went slack as she realized that a simple flounce from the table had been transformed into total eviction. Closing her mouth with a snap, she turned to glare at Justin. "Are you going to allow an insolent American hussy to drive me from my own home?"

Justin looked from his mother to his wife, acute discomfort on his face. Silently Sunny pleaded with him to support her. He had said that she was the mistress of Swindon. If he didn't back her now, her position would become intolerable.

"You've been complaining that the new central heating gives you headaches, Mother," Justin said expressionlessly. "I think it an excellent idea for you to move to the Dower House so that you will be more comfortable. We shall miss you, of course, but fortunately you won't be far away."

Sunny shut her eyes for an instant, almost undone by relief. When she opened them again, the dowager's venomous gaze had gone to her daughter. "The Dower House isn't large enough for me to have Alexandra underfoot," she said waspishly. "She shall have to stay in the palace."

Before her mother-in-law could reconsider, Sunny said warmly, "Very true. Until she marries, Alexandra belongs at Swindon."

"If she ever marries," the dowager said viciously. Knowing that she was defeated and that the only way to salvage her dignity was to pretend that moving was her own idea, she added, "You shall have to learn to run the household yourself, Sarah, for I have been longing to travel. I believe I shall spend the rest of the winter in southern France. England is so dismal at this season." Ramrod straight, she marched from the room.

Sunny, Justin and Alexandra were left sitting in brittle silence. Not daring to meet her husband's eyes, Sunny said, "I'm sorry if I was disrespectful to your mother, but... but I'm not sorry for what I said!"

"That's a contradiction in terms," he said, sounding sad and weary, but not angry. Changing the subject, he continued, "By the way, I saw Lord Hopstead in London, and he invited us for a weekend visit and ball at Cottenham. I thought the three of us could go, then you could take Alexandra on to Paris for her fittings."

Relieved that he didn't refer to her confrontation with the dowager, Sunny said, "That sounds delightful. Are you ready for your first ball, Alexandra? I have a gown that will look marvelous on you with only minor alterations."

"That's very kind of you," a subdued Alexandra said.

For several minutes, they stiffly discussed the proposed trip, none of them making any allusion to the dowager's rout. It was like ignoring the fact that an elephant was in the room.

Finally Sunny got to her feet. "I'm very tired tonight.

If you two will excuse me, I'll go to bed now." Her temples throbbed as she climbed to her room, but under her shakiness, she was triumphant. Without the dowager's poisonous presence, life at Swindon would improve remarkably.

She changed to her nightgown and slipped into bed, wondering if Justin would visit her. Ordinarily he did after returning from a journey, but perhaps he would stay away if he was displeased with the way she had treated his mother.

Though it shamed her to admit it, she had come to look forward to his conjugal visits. One particular night stood out in her mind. She had been drifting in the misty zone between sleep and waking when her husband came. Though aware of his presence, she had been too drowsy to move her languid limbs.

Instead of waking her, he had given a small sigh, then stretched out beside her, his warm body against hers, his quiet breath caressing her temple. After several minutes he began stroking her, his hand gliding gently over her torso.

She had lain utterly still, embarrassed by the yearning sensations that tingled in her breasts and other unmentionable places. Pleasure thickened inside her until she had had to bite her lip to keep from moaning and moving against his hand.

Fortunately, before she disgraced herself he dozed off, his hand cupping her breast. Slowly her tension had dissipated until she also slept.

Her rest was remarkably deep, considering that she had never in her life shared a bed with another person. But when she awoke the next morning, he was gone.

She might have thought she'd dreamed the episode if not for the imprint of her husband's head on the pillow and a faint, lingering masculine scent. It had occurred to her that people who could not afford to have separate bedrooms might be luckier than they knew.

But she was mortified by the knowledge that she had the nature of a wanton. The next time she saw Katie Westron, she must find the boldness to ask how a woman could control her carnality, for surely Katie would know.

Until then, Sunny would simply have to exercise willpower. She could almost hear her mother saying, "You are a lady. Behave like one."

Yet still she longed for her husband's company. She had almost given up hope that he would join her when the connecting door quietly opened and he padded across the deep carpet As he slipped into the bed, she touched his arm to show that she was awake and willing. He slid his hand beneath the covers and drew up the hem of her nightgown.

Perhaps the evening's drama was affecting her, for she found it particularly difficult to keep silent while he prepared her for intercourse. Those strange feelings that were part pleasure, part pain, fluttered through her as he smoothed lotion over her sensitive female parts.

When he entered her, heat pulsed through those same parts, then expanded to other parts of her body. She caught her breath, unable to entirely suppress her reaction.

Immediately he stopped moving. "Did I hurt you?"

"N-no." She knotted her hands and pressed her limbs rigidly into the mattress. "No, you didn't hurt me."

Gently he began rocking back and forth again. The slowness of his movements caused deeply disquieting sensations. Yet curiously , instead of wanting them to stop, she wanted more. It was hard, so hard, to be still....

His breathing quickened in the way that told her that the end was near. He gave a muffled groan and made a final deep thrust. Then his tension ebbed away.

She felt a corresponding easing in herself, as if her feelings were intertwined with his. She was tempted to slide her arms around him, for she had a most unladylike desire to keep his warm, hard body pressed tightly against her. Perhaps he might fall asleep with her again.

But that was not what men and women of good breeding did. Her parents had not shared a room. After Sunny's birth, they had probably not even had conjugal relations, for she was the youngest in the family. Once her father had two sons to work in the business and her mother had a daughter for companionship, there had been no need for more babies.

Justin lifted his weight from her. After pulling her gown down again, he lightly touched her hair. She wanted to catch his hand and beg him to stay, but of course she didn't.

Then he left her.

When the connecting door between their chambers closed, Sunny released her breath in a shuddering sigh, then rolled over and hugged a pillow to her chest She felt restless impatience and a kind of itchy discomfort in her female parts. Her hand slid down her torso. Perhaps if she rubbed herself there...

Horrified, she flopped onto her back and clenched her hands into fists. Her nurse and her mother had made it clear that a woman never touched herself "down there" unless she had to.

She closed her eyes against the sting of tears. She was trying her very best to be a good wife. But from what she could see, a good wife was a lonely woman.

§

*I*n a flurry of trunks and contradictory orders, the Dowager Duchess of Thornborough moved herself and a substantial number of Swindon's finest antiques to the elegant Dower House on the far side of the estate.

Then she promptly decamped to the French Riviera, there to flaunt her rank and make slanderous hints about her son's inadequacies and her daughter-in-law's insolence. The one thing Justin was sure she would not say was the truth: that a slip of an American girl had maneuvered the dowager out of Swindon Palace.

Life was much easier with his mother gone. He and Sunny and Alexandra dined *en famille*, with much less formality and far more enjoyment. His sister was blossoming under Sunny's kind guidance, and no longer dreaded her social debut.

What wasn't prospering was his marriage. Ever since his incredibly clumsy remark about sparing future dukes the necessity of marrying for money, there had been strain between him and Sunny. What he had meant was that he wanted financial considerations to be irrelevant.

Unfortunately, she had believed the unintended insult rather than his heartfelt declaration that he would have wanted to marry her anyhow. Because he had accidentally hurt her, she had struck back, hurting him in return when she had underlined the fact that their marriage had nothing to do with love.

Fearing that more explanations would only make matters worse, he hadn't raised the subject again. Eventually memory of the incident would fade, but in the meantime Sunny had pulled further away from him. She was courteous, compliant—and as distant as if an ocean still divided them.

Sometimes she trembled during their wordless conjugal couplings, and he feared that she was recoiling from his touch. If she had verbally objected, perhaps he could have controlled his desires and stopped inflicting himself on her. But she said nothing, and he did not have the strength to stay away.

As they prepared to go to the ball at Cottenham Manor, he hoped that Sunny's return to society would cheer her. She deserved laughter and frivolity and admiration.

Yet though he wanted her to be happy, the knowledge that she would be surrounded by adoring, predatory men terrified him. If she was miserable in her marriage, how long would it be before she looked elsewhere?

If you would be troubled, take a wife.

CHAPTER 8

Cottenham Manor
March 1886

Cottenham Manor, seat of the Earl of Hopstead, was almost as grand and large as Swindon Palace. Lord and Lady Hopstead were famous for their entertainments, and Sunny had spent a long and happy weekend at Cottenham the previous summer. It was a pleasure to return, and as her maid fastened a sapphire and diamond necklace around her neck, she hummed softly to herself.

"Madam is happy tonight," Antoinette observed as she handed Sunny the matching eardrops.

Sunny put on the eardrops, then turned her head so she could see the play of light in the sapphire pendants. "I've been looking forward to this ball for weeks. What a silly custom it is for a bride to rusticate for months after the wedding!"

"But think how much more you will appreciate society after wintering in the depths of the English countryside."

"That's true." Sunny rose with a rich whisper of taffeta petticoats. She was wearing a sumptuous blue brocade gown, one of Worth's finest, and she was ready to be admired.

"You must sit until I have put on your tiara," Antoinette said reprovingly.

Obediently Sunny sat again and braced herself for the weight of the Thornborough tiara. The massive, diamond-studded coronet would give her a headache, but it wouldn't be proper for a duchess to attend a ball without one, particularly since the Prince of Wales would be present.

Just as the maid was finishing, a hesitant knock sounded at the door. Antoinette crossed the room and admitted Alexandra. Dressed in a white silk gown that shimmered with every movement, the younger girl had a fairylike grace. Her dark hair had been swept up to show the delicate line of her throat, and her complexion glowed with youth and good health.

"You look marvelous," Sunny said warmly. "Turn around so I can see all of you."

Her sister-in-law colored prettily as she obeyed. "You were right about the gown. Even though this one wasn't made for me, it's so lovely that one can't help but feel beautiful."

"It looks better on you than it ever did on me. You'll be the belle of the ball."

"No, you will." Alexandra chuckled. "But at least I don't think that I'll be a wallflower." Another knock sounded on the door. This time it was Justin, come to take his wife and sister down to the dinner that would precede the ball. Sunny had hoped that there would be so many people at

Cottenham that they would be put in the same room, but such intimacy was unthinkable in the fashionable set. The previous night, she had slept alone. Perhaps tonight…

Hastily she suppressed the improper thought. After he examined them both, Justin said gravely, "You will be the two most beautiful women at the ball. Alex, I shall have a dozen men clamoring for your hand before the evening is over."

As Alexandra beamed delightedly, he offered one arm to his wife and one to his sister, then led them into the hall. As they descended the broad stairs, Sunny asked, "Will you dance with me tonight?"

He gave her a quizzical glance. "You would dance with a mere husband?"

"Please." Afraid that she might sound pathetic, she added lightly, "I know that it's not fashionable to dance with one's spouse, but it isn't actually scandalous."

He gave her one of the rare smiles that took her breath away. "Then it will be my very great pleasure."

As they entered the salon where the other guests had gathered, Sunny's heart was already dancing.

❧

The Hopsteads' ball was an excellent place to rejoin society, and Sunny enjoyed greeting people she had met the year before. During a break after the fourth dance, she came across her godmother, who was resplendent in coral-and-silver silk. "Aunt Katie!" Sunny gave her a hug. "I hoped you would be here. You're not staying at Cottenham, are you?"

"No, I'm at the Howards'. Every great house in the district is full of guests who have come for this ball." Katie affectionately tucked a tendril of Sunny's flyaway hair in place. "You're in fine looks. By any chance are you...?"

"Please, don't ask me if I'm expecting a blessed event! I swear, every female at the ball has inquired. I'm beginning to feel like a dreadful failure."

"Nonsense. You've only been married a few months." Katie chuckled. "It's just that we're all such gossips, and like it or not, you're a subject of great interest."

Sunny made a face. "Luckily there will soon be other heiresses to capture society's attention." The two women chatted for a few minutes and made an engagement for the next morning.

Then Sunny glanced beyond Katie, and her heart froze in her breast. On the far side of the room was Paul Curzon, tall and distinguished and heart-stoppingly handsome.

As if feeling her gaze, he looked up, and for a paralyzing instant their eyes met. Shocked by the way her knees weakened, Sunny turned to Katie and stammered, "I must go now. I'll see you tomorrow."

Then she caught her train up with one hand and headed for the nearest door, scarcely noticing when she bumped into other guests. Sometimes escape was more important than manners.

ভ

One of the drawbacks of socializing was the number of people who hoped to enlist ducal support for some cause or other. This time, it was a junior government minister talking about an upcoming bill. Justin listened patiently, half of his attention on the minister, the other half anticipating the next dance, which would be with Sunny.

Then from the corner of his eye, he saw his wife leave the ballroom, her face pale. He frowned, wondering if she was feeling ill.

He was about to excuse himself when he saw Paul Curzon go out the same side door that Sunny had used. Justin's face stiffened as a horrible suspicion seized him.

Seeing his expression, the minister said earnestly, "I swear, your grace, the scheme is perfectly sound. If you wish, I'll show you the figures."

Justin realized that he couldn't even remember what the damned bill was about. Brusquely he said, "Send me the information and I'll give you my decision in a week."

Hoping desperately that he was wrong, he brushed aside the minister's thanks and made his way after his wife and the man whom she might still love.

&

*S*unny chose the conservatory for her refuge. It was at the opposite end of the house from the ball, and as she had hoped, she had it to herself.

Cottenham was noted for its magnificent indoor garden, and scattered gaslights illuminated banks of flowers and lush tropical shrubbery. Though rain drummed on the glass panels far above her head, inside the air was balmy and richly scented.

She took a deep breath, then set out along one of the winding brick paths. It had been foolish to become upset at the sight of Paul Curzon, for she had known that inevitably they would meet. But she had not expected it to be tonight. If she had been mentally prepared, she would have been able to accept his presence with equanimity.

Yet honesty compelled her to admit that in the first

instant, she had felt some of the excitement she had known in the days when she had loved him. In the days when she *thought* she loved him, before she had discovered his baseness.

As always, nature helped her regain her composure. If she hadn't been dressed in a ball gown, she would have looked for some plants to repot. Instead, she picked a gardenia blossom and inhaled the delicate perfume.

As she did, a familiar voice said huskily, "The conservatory was a perfect choice, darling. No one will see us here."

"Paul!" The shock was as great as when she had first seen him, and spasmodically she crushed the gardenia blossom in her palm. After a fierce struggle for control, she turned and said evenly, "I didn't come here to meet you, Paul, but to get away from you. We have nothing to say to each other."

Unfortunately the way out lay past him. As she tried to slip by without her broad skirts touching him, he caught her hand. "Sunny, don't go yet," he begged. "I'm sorry if I misunderstood why you came here, but I wanted so much to see you that hope warped my judgment. I made the worst mistake of my life with you! At least give me a chance to apologize."

Reluctantly she stopped, as much because of the narrow aisle as because of his words. "I'm not interested in your apologies." As she spoke, she looked into his face, which was a mistake. He didn't look base; he looked sincere, and sinfully handsome.

"If you won't let me apologize, then let me say how much I love you." A tremor sounded in his voice. "I truly didn't know how much until I lost you."

Reminding herself that he had looked equally honest before he had broken her heart, she tried to free her hand, saying tartly, "Perhaps you think that you love me because you lost me. Isn't that how people like you play at love?"

His grip tightened. "This is different! The fact that you were willing to marry me is the greatest honor I've ever known. But I let myself be blinded by worldly considerations, and now I'm paying for my folly. Both of us are."

"There's no point in talking like this! The past can't be changed, and I'm a married woman now."

"Perhaps the past can't be changed, but the future can be." He put his hand under her chin and turned her face to his. "Love is too precious to throw away."

His gaze holding hers, he pressed his heated lips to her gloved fingers. "You are so beautiful, Sunny. I have never loved a woman as much as I love you."

She knew that she should break away, for she didn't love him, didn't trust his protestations of devotion. Yet her parched heart yearned for warmth, for words of love, even ones that might be false.

Her inner struggle held her paralyzed as he put his arms around her and bent his head for a kiss. In a moment, she would push him away and leave. Yet even though it was wrong, for just an instant she would let him hold her....

&

*T*he conservatory seemed like the most likely spot for dalliance, but Justin had only been there once, and he lost precious time with a wrong turn. His heart was pounding with fear when he finally reached his destination and threw open the door.

He paused on the threshold and scanned the shadowy garden, praying that he was wrong. But through the dense vegetation, he saw a shimmering patch of blue the shade of

Sunny's gown. Down a brick path, around a bend... and he found his wife in Paul Curzon's arms.

The pain was worse than anything Justin had ever known. For a moment he stood stock-still as nausea pulsed through him. Then came rage. Stalking forward, he snarled, "If you expect me to be a complaisant husband, you're both fools."

The two broke apart instantly, and Sunny whirled to him, her face white. Justin grabbed her wrist and pulled her away from Curzon. Then he looked his rival in the eye and said with lethal precision, "If you ever come near my wife again, I will destroy you."

"No need to carry on so, old man," Curzon said hastily. "It was merely a friendly kiss between acquaintances."

Justin's free hand knotted into a fist. "*I will destroy you!*"

As Curzon paled, Justin turned and swept his wife away, heedless of the difficulty that she had keeping up in her high-heeled kid slippers. When she stumbled, his grip tightened to keep her from falling, but he did not slow down.

Wanting to ease the rage in his face, she said desperately, "Justin, that wasn't what you think." He gave her a piercing glance. "It looked very much like a kiss to me. Am I wrong?"

"Yes, but... but it didn't really mean anything."

"If kisses mean nothing to you, does that mean you'll give them to any man?" he asked bitterly. "Or only those with whom you have assignations?"

"You're deliberately misunderstanding me! I went to the conservatory to avoid Paul, not to meet him. I know that I shouldn't have let him kiss me, but it was just a... a temporary aberration that happened only because there were once...warmer feelings between us."

"And if I hadn't come, they would have become warmer yet. If I had been ten minutes later..." His voice broke.

Guilt rose in a choking wave. Though she had not sought the encounter with Paul, she had not left when she should, and she had allowed him to kiss her. Might the warmth of Paul's embrace have dissolved her knowledge of right and wrong?

She wanted to believe that morality would have triumphed, but treacherous doubt gnawed at her. Since she had discovered her wanton nature, she could no longer trust herself.

They reached the hallway below the main staircase. Several couples were enjoying the cooler air there, and they all turned to stare at the duke and duchess. Dropping her voice, Sunny hissed, "Let go of me! What will people think?"

"I don't give a tinker's dam what anyone thinks." He began climbing the staircase, still holding tightly to her wrist to keep her at his side. "Your behavior is what concerns me."

He followed the upstairs corridor to her bedchamber, pulled her inside, then slammed the door behind them and turned the key in the lock. The room was empty, lit only by the soft glow of a gas lamp. She edged uneasily away, for this furious man was a stranger, and he was starting to frighten her.

They stared at each other across the width of the room. With the same lethal intensity he had directed at Paul, Justin growled, "In the Middle Ages, I could have locked you in a tower or a chastity belt. A century ago, I could have challenged any man who came near you to a duel. But what can a man do about a faithless wife in these the times?"

His words triggered her secret fear. "What about faithless husbands?" she retorted. "I've been told that men like you always have mistresses. Is the real reason for your trips to London another woman? One that you couldn't have because you had to many for money?"

Renewed fury blazed in his gray eyes, and a dark hunger. "I have not looked at—or touched—anyone else since I met you. I wish to God that you could say the same! But since you choose to act like a whore, I will treat you as one." He swept across the room and shattered her with a kiss.

Sunny had thought that her months of marriage had educated her about what happened between husband and wife, but nothing had prepared her for Justin's embrace. The quiet consideration to which she was accustomed had been replaced by blazing rage.

Trapped in the prison of his arms, she was acutely aware of his strength. Even if she wanted to resist, any effort on her part would be futile. Yet as they stood locked together, his mouth devouring hers, she sensed that his fury was changing into something that was similar, but was not anger at all. And it called to her.

Her head tilted and the heavy tiara pulled loose and fell to the carpet, jerking sharply at her hair. When she winced, his crushing grip eased and he began stroking her head with one hand. His deft fingers found and soothed the hurt. She didn't realize that he was also removing the pins until coils of hair cascaded over her shoulders.

He buried his face in the silken mass, and she felt the beating of his heart and the soft exhalation of his breath against her cheek. "Dear God, Sunny!" he said with anguish. "You are so beautiful. So painfully beautiful."

Yet his expression was harsh when he straightened and turned her so that her back was to him. First he unhooked her sapphire necklace, throwing it aside as if it was a piece of cut-glass trumpery. Then he started to unfasten her gown.

She opened her mouth to object, but before she could, he pressed his mouth to the side of her throat. With lips and tongue, he found sensitivities she hadn't known she possessed. As he trailed tiny, nibbling kisses down her neck and along her shoulder, she released her breath in a shuddering sigh, all thoughts of protest chased from her mind. Potent awareness curled through her, pooling hotly in unmentionable places.

When the gown was undone, he pushed it off her shoulders and down her arms. The rough warmth of his fingers made an erotic contrast to the cool silk that skimmed her flesh in a feather-light caress, then slithered in a rush to the floor, leaving her in her under things. Instinctively she raised her hands to cover her breasts, stammering, "Th-this is highly improper."

"You have forfeited the right to talk about propriety." He untied her layered crinolette petticoat and dragged it down around her ankles. Then he began unlacing her blue satin corset. Stays were a lady's armor against impropriety, and she stood rigidly still, horribly aware that every inch of her newly liberated flesh burned with life and longing.

Then, shockingly, he slid his hands under the loose corset and cupped her breasts, using his thumbs to tease her nipples through the thin fabric of her chemise. It was like the time he had caressed her when he thought her asleep, but a thousand times more intense. Unable to suppress her reaction, she shuddered and rolled her hips against him.

"You like that, my lady trollop?" he murmured in her ear.

She wanted to deny it but couldn't. Her limbs weakened

and she wilted against him, mindlessly reveling in the waves of sensation that flooded through her. The firm support of his broad chest, the silken tease of his tongue on the edge of her ear, the exquisite pleasure that expanded from her breasts to encompass her entire being, coiling tighter and tighter deep inside her....

She did not come to her senses until he tossed aside her corset and turned her to face him. Horrified by her lewd response and her near nakedness, she stumbled away from the pile of crumpled clothing and retreated until her back was to the wall. "I have never shirked my wifely duty," she said feebly, "but this... this isn't right!"

"Tonight, right is what I say it is." His implacable gaze holding hers, he stripped off his own clothing with brusque, impatient movements. "And this time, I will have you naked and in the light."

She could not take her eyes away as he removed his formal garments to reveal the hard, masculine body beneath. The well-defined muscles that rippled beneath his skin. The dark hair that patterned his chest and arrowed down his belly. And the arrogant male organ, which she had felt but never seen.

She stared for an instant both mortified and fascinated, then blushed violently and closed her eyes. No wonder decent couples had marital relations in the dark, for the sight of a man's body was profoundly disturbing.

A Vienna waltz was playing in the distance. She had trouble believing that under this same roof hundreds of people were laughing and flirting and playing society's games. Compared to the devastating reality of Justin, the outside world had no more substance than shadows.

Even with her eyes closed, she was acutely aware of his nakedness when he drew her into his arms again, surrounding her with heat and maleness. Her breath came rapid and irregular as he peeled away the last frail protection of chemise, drawers and stockings. His fingers left trails of fire as they brushed her limbs and torso.

She inhaled sharply when he swept her into his arms and laid her across the bed, his taut frame pinning her to the mattress. Though she tried to control her shameful reactions, she moaned with pleasure when his mouth claimed her breast with arrant carnality.

No matter how hard she tried, she could not lie still as he caressed and kissed and tasted her, the velvet stroke of his tongue driving her to madness. His masterful touch abraded away every layer of decorum until she no longer remembered, or cared, how a lady should act. In the shameless turmoil of intimacy, she was tinder to his flame.

She was lovely beyond his dreams, and everything about her intoxicated him. The haunting lure of wild violets, her tangled sun-struck hair, the lush eroticism of removing layer after layer of clothing until finally her flawless body was revealed. Her lithe, feminine grace wrenched his heart.

Yet side by side with tenderness, he found savage satisfaction in her choked whimpers of pleasure. His wife might be a duchess and a lady, but for tonight, at least, she was a woman, and she was his.

This time there would be no need of lotion to ease their joining. She was hotly ready, and she writhed against his hand as he caressed the moist, delicate folds of female flesh. Her moan gave him a deep sense of masculine pride, dissolving the aching emptiness he had known in their inhibited marriage bed.

When he could no longer bear his separateness, he entered her. The voluptuous welcome of her body was exquisite, both torment and homecoming. Trembling with strain, he forced himself to move with slow deliberation. This time he would not let their union end too quickly.

Vivid emotions rippled across her sweat-sheened face. But he wanted more; he wanted communion of the mind as well as the body. He wanted acknowledgment of the power he had over her. Hoarsely he asked, "Do you desire me?"

"You... you are my husband." She turned her head to the side, as if trying to evade his question. "It is my duty to comply with your wishes."

Mere obedience was not what he wanted from his wife. He repeated more intensely, "Do you desire me?" Slowly, by infinitesimal degrees, he began to withdraw. "If not, perhaps I should stop now."

"No!" she gasped, her eyes flying open for an instant and her body arching sharply upward. "Don't leave me, please. I couldn't bear it..."

It was what he had longed to hear. He responded to her admission by surrendering to the fiery need that bound them. No longer passive, she was his partner in passion, her nails slashing his back as they thrust against each other. She cried out with ecstasy as long, shuddering convulsions rocked them both, and in the culmination of desire he felt their soaring spirits blend.

In the tremulous aftermath, he gathered her pliant body into his arms and tucked the covers around them. As they dozed off together, he knew they had truly become husband and wife.

&.

Justin was not sure how long he had slept. The ball must have ended, for he could no longer hear music and laughter, but the sky outside was still dark. He lay on his side with Sunny nestled along him, her face against his shoulder.

Not wanting to wake her, he touched the luscious tangle of her hair with a gossamer caress. He had never known such happiness, or such peace. Not only was she the loveliest and sweetest of women, but she was blessed with an ardent nature. If he hadn't been so blasted deferential, he would have discovered that much sooner. But now that they had found each other, their lives would be different.

Her eyes opened and gazed into his. For a long moment, they simply stared at each other. He stroked the elegant curve of her back and prepared to make the declaration of love that he had never made to any other woman.

But she spoke first, saying in a thin, exhausted voice, "Who *are* you?"

A chill touched his heart as he wondered if she was out of her senses, but she seemed lucid. Warily he replied, "Your husband, of course."

She gave a tiny shake of her head. "You are more a stranger to me now than on the day we married."

He looked away, unable to face the dazed bleakness in her aqua eyes. He had known that she had not yet been unfaithful; she not the sort of woman to engage lightly in an affair, and buried at Swindon she hadn't even had an opportunity. Yet seeing her in Curzon's arms had devastated Justin because it was a horrific preview of the possibility that he would lose her.

Despair had made him furiously determined to show her what fulfillment was. He had wanted to possess her, body and soul, to make her his own so profoundly that she would never look at another man. He realized that he had also hoped to win her love by demonstrating the depth of his passion.

But the fact that he had been able to arouse her latent ardor did not mean that she suddenly, miraculously loved him. With sickening clarity, he saw that in his anger he had ruthlessly stripped away her dignity and modesty. Instead of liberating her passion, he had ravished her spirit, turning her into a broken shadow of the happy girl who had first captured his heart.

His unspoken words of love withered and died.

Instead he said painfully, "I am no different now from what I was then."

He wanted to say more, to apologize and beg her forgiveness, but she turned away and buried her face in the pillows. Feeling that he would shatter if he moved too suddenly, he slid from the bed and numbly dragged on enough clothing to make his way the short distance to his room.

As he left, he wondered despairingly if he would ever be able to face his wife again.

CHAPTER 9

*S*unny awoke the next morning churning with tangled emotions. The only thing she knew for certain was that she could not bear to face a house full of avid-eyed, curious people. With a groan, she rolled over, buried her head under a pillow and did her best not to think.

But her mind refused to cooperate. She could not stop herself from wondering where Justin was and what he thought of the events of the previous night She was mortified by memories of her wantonness, and angry with her husband for making her behave so badly. But though she tried to cling to anger over his disrespect, other things kept seeping into her mind. Memories of heartwarming closeness, and shattering excitement....

At that point in her thoughts, her throat always tightened. Justin had said he would treat her as a whore, and her response had confirmed his furious accusation.

For the first time in her life, Sunny understand why a woman might choose to go into a nunnery. A world with no men would be infinitely simpler.

Eventually Antoinette tiptoed into the dim, heavily curtained room. "Madame is not feeling well this morning?"

"Madame has a ghastly headache. I wish to be left alone." Remembering her obligations, Sunny added, "Tell Lady Alexandra not to be concerned about me. I'm sure I'll be fine by dinner."

There was a long silence. Even with her eyes closed, Sunny knew that her maid was surveying the disordered bedchamber and probably drawing accurate conclusions.

Tactful Antoinette said only, "After I straighten the room, I shall leave. Perhaps later you would like tea and toast?"

"Perhaps."

As the maid quietly tidied up the evidence of debauchery, someone knocked on the door and handed in a message. After the footman left, Antoinette said, "Monsieur le Due has sent a note." Sunny came tensely awake. "Leave it on the table."

After the maid left, Sunny sat up in bed and stared at the letter as if it were a poisonous serpent. Then she swung her feet to the floor. Only then did she realize that she was stark naked. Worse, her body showed unaccustomed marks where sensitive skin had been nipped, or rasped by a whiskered masculine face. And her body would not be the only one marked this morning....

Face flushed, she darted to the armoire and grabbed the first nightgown and wrapper she saw. After she was decently covered, she brushed her wild hair into submission and pulled it into a severe knot When she could delay no longer, she opened the waiting envelope.

She was not sure what she expected, but the scrawled words, *"I'm sorry. Thornborough"* were a painful letdown. What was her husband sorry about? Their marriage? His wife's appallingly wanton nature? His own disproportionate rage, which had led him to humiliate her?

The use of his title rather than his Christian name was blunt proof that the moments of intimacy she had imagined the night before were an illusion. Crumpling the note in one hand, she buried her face in her hands and struggled against tears.

The wretched circle of her thoughts was interrupted by another knock. Though she called out, "I do not wish for company," the door swung open anyhow.

In walked Katie Westron, immaculately dressed in a morning gown and with a tray in her hands. "It's past noon, and you and I were engaged to take a drive an hour ago."

She set the tray down and surveyed her goddaughter. "You look quite dreadful, my dear, and they say that Thornborough left Cottenham this morning at dawn, looking like death."

So he was gone. Apparently he couldn't bear being under the same roof with her any longer. Trying to mask the pain of that thought, Sunny asked, "Are people talking?"

"Some, though not as much as they were before I said that Thornborough had always intended to leave today because he had business at Swindon." Briskly Katie opened the draperies so that light flooded the room. "And as I pointed out, who wouldn't look exhausted after a late night at such a delightful ball?"

"He was planning to leave early, but not until tomorrow." Sunny managed a wry half smile. "You lie beautifully."

"It's a prime social skill." Katie prepared two cups of coffee and handed one to Sunny, then took the other and perched on the window seat. "There's nothing like coffee to put one's troubles in perspective. Have a ginger cake, too, they're very good." After daintily biting one, Katie continued, "Would you like to tell me why you and Thornborough both look so miserable?"

The scalding coffee did clear Sunny's mind. She was in dire need of the advice of an older and wiser woman, and she would find no kinder or more tolerant listener than her godmother.

Haltingly she described her marriage: the distance between her and her husband, her loneliness, her encounter with Paul Curzon and the shocking result. Of the last she said very little, and that with her face burning, but she suspected that her godmother could make a shrewd guess about what went unsaid. At the end, she asked, "What do you think?"

"Exactly why are you so upset?" Katie asked bluntly

After long thought, Sunny said slowly, "I don't understand my marriage, my husband or myself. In particular, I find Justin incomprehensible. Before, I thought he was polite but basically indifferent to me. Now I think he must despise me, or he would never have treated me with such disrespect."

Katie bit into another cake. "Do you wish to end the marriage?"

"Of course I don't want a divorce!"

"Why 'of course'? There would be a ghastly scandal, and some social circles exclude all divorced women, but as a Vangelder, you would be able to weather that."

Sunny sorted through her tangled thoughts. "It would be humiliating for Thornborough. If I left him, people would think that he mistreated me horribly."

Katie's brows arched. "Aren't you saying that he did exactly that?"

"In most ways, he's been very considerate." She thought of the bathroom that he had had installed for her, and almost smiled. Not the most romantic gift, perhaps, but one that gave her daily pleasure.

"You'd be a fool to live in misery simply to save Thornborough embarrassment," Katie said tartly. "A little singed pride will be good for him, and as a duke he will certainly not be ruined socially. He can find another wife with a snap of his fingers. The next one might not be able to match your dowry, but that's all right. The Swindon roof has already been replaced, and you can hardly take it back. What matters is that you'll be free to find a more congenial husband."

The thought of Justin with another wife made Sunny's hackles rise. "I don't want another husband." She bit her lip. "In fact, I can't imagine being married to anyone else. It would seem wrong. Immoral."

"Oh?" Katie said with interest "What is so special about Thornborough? From what you say, he's a dull sort of fellow, and he's not particularly good-looking."

"He's not dull! He's kind, intelligent and very witty, even though he's quiet. He has a sense of responsibility, which many men in his position don't. And he's really quite attractive. Not in a sleek, fashionable way, but very... very manly."

Her godmother smiled gently. "You sound like a woman who is in love with her husband."

"I do?" Sunny tried the idea on, and was shocked to realize that it was true. She was happy in Justin's presence. On some deep level that had nothing to do with their current problems, she trusted him. "But he doesn't love or respect me. Last night he said that since I had behaved like a... a woman of no virtue, he would treat me like one." A vivid memory of his mouth on her breast caused her to blush again.

"Did he hurt you?"

"No, but he... offended my modesty." Sunny stared at her hands, unable to meet her godmother's gaze. "In fairness, I must admit that I did not behave as properly as I should. I was... shocked to discover how wantonly I could behave."

"In other words, your husband made passionate love to you, you found it entrancing as well as alarming, and are now ashamed of yourself."

The color drained from Sunny's face, leaving her white. "How did you know?"

Setting aside her coffee cup, Katie said, "The time has come to speak frankly. I suppose that your mother told you that no decent woman ever enjoyed her marriage bed, and that discreet suffering was the mark of a lady."

When her goddaughter nod, Katie continued, "There are many who agree with her, but another school of opinion says that there is nothing wrong with taking pleasure in the bodies that the good Lord gave us. What is the Song of Solomon but a hymn to the joy of physical and spiritual love?"

Weakly Sunny said, "Mother would say you're talking blasphemy."

"Augusta is one of my oldest and dearest friends, but she and your father were ill-suited, and naturally that has affected her views on marital relations." Katie leaned forward earnestly. "Satisfaction in the marriage bed binds a couple together, and the better a woman pleases her husband, the less likely he is to stray. And vice versa, I might add." She cocked her head. "If you hadn't been raised to believe that conjugal pleasure was immodest, would you have enjoyed the passion and intimacy that you experienced last night?"

The idea of reveling in carnality was so shocking that it

took Sunny's breath away, yet it was also powerfully compelling. She had come to look forward to Justin's visits and to long for more of his company. The idea that her response was natural, not wanton, was heady indeed.

More memories of the previous night's explosive passion burned across her brain. Though the episode had been upsetting, there had also been moments of stunning emotional intimacy, when she and her husband had seemed to be one flesh and one spirit. If such intensity could be woven into the fabric of a marriage, it would bind a man and woman together for as long as they lived. And if passion made a marriage stronger, surely fulfillment could not be truly wicked.

There was only one problem. "I'd like to think that you're right, but what does it matter if I love my husband and he holds me in contempt? Justin has never said a single word of love."

Katie smiled wryly. "Englishmen are taught to conceal their emotions in the nursery, and the more deeply they care, the harder it is for them to speak. In my experience, the men who talk most easily of love are those who have had entirely too much practice. The more sparingly a man gives his heart, the more precious the gift, and the less adept he is at declarations of love. But deeds matter more than words, and an ounce of genuine caring is worth a pound of smooth, insincere compliments."

Abruptly Sunny remembered that Justin had said that he hadn't looked at another woman since meeting her. She had thought that was merely a riposte in their argument, but if true, it might be an oblique declaration of love. Hesitantly she said, "Do you think it's possible that Justin loves me?"

"You would know that better than I. But he seems the

sort who would be more of a doer than a talker." Katie's brows drew together. "Men are simple creatures, and for them, love and passion often get knotted up together. If he does love you in a passionate way, the kind of restrained marriage you have described must be difficult for him."

And if he was finding the marriage difficult, he would withdraw; that much Sunny knew about her husband. She had regretted the fact that he had never reached out to her with affection, yet neither had she ever reached out to him. Perhaps she was as much responsible for the distance between them as he was.

Attempting lightness, she said, "I suppose the way to find out how he feels about me is to hand him my heart on a platter, then see whether he accepts it or chops it into little pieces."

"I'm afraid so." Katie shook her head ruefully. "All marriages have ups and downs, particularly in the early years. I was once in a situation a bit like yours, where I had to risk what could have been a humiliating rejection. It wasn't easy to humble myself, but the results were worth it." She smiled. "A witty vicar once said that a good marriage is like a pair of scissors with the couple inseparably joined, often moving in opposite directions, yet always destroying anyone who comes between them. The trick is for the blades to learn to work smoothly together, so as not to cut each other."

That's what Sunny and Justin had been doing: cutting each other. Feeling a century older than she had the day before, Sunny gave a shaky smile. "Apparently I must learn to speak with American bluntness."

"That's the spirit! But first, you might want to ask yourself what you want out of your marriage."

"Love, companionship, children. I don't want to withdraw entirely from society, but the fashionable world will never be the center of my life, the way it is for my mother." Her brow wrinkled. "Perhaps if my parents had been happier together, my father would not have worked so hard, and my mother would not have cared as much about society."

"I've often suspected that many of the world's most dazzling achievements are a result of a miserable domestic situation." Katie considered. "You might want to wait until both you and Thornborough have had time to recover from what was obviously a distressing episode. You were about to take Alexandra to Paris, weren't you? In your place, I would carry on with my original plans. That will give you time to think and decide exactly how to proceed."

"I'm going to need it." Sunny rose and hugged her godmother. "Thank you, Aunt Katie. What can I do to repay you?"

"When you're old and wise like me, you can give worldly advice to other confused young ladies." Katie smiled reminiscently. "Which is exactly what I was told by an eccentric, sharp-tongued Westron aunt who sent me back to my husband when I was a bewildered bride."

Sunny nodded gravely. "I promise to pass on whatever womanly wisdom I acquire."

But before she was in a position to give good advice, she must fix her own frayed marriage. And that, she knew, would be easier said than done.

CHAPTER 10

*A*lexandra looked eagerly from the carriage window. "Almost home! It's hard to believe that it's been only a month since we left Swindon. I feel years older."

Sunny smiled, trying to conceal her nerves. "Paris has that effect on people. You really have changed, too. You left as a girl and are returning as a young woman."

"I hope so." Alexandra grinned. "But I'm going to go right up to my room and take off my wonderful Worth travel ensemble. Then I'll curl up in my window seat and read that new Rider Haggard novel I bought in London. Though Paris was wonderful, there's nothing quite like a good book."

"You've earned the right to a little self-indulgence." Sunny gave her sister-in-law a fond smile. Petite and pretty, Alexandra would never be called the Gargoylette again, and the difference was more than mere clothing. Now that Alexandra was free of her mother's crushing influence, she was developing poise, confidence and a quiet charm that would surely win her whatever man she eventually honored with her heart.

The carriage pulled up in front of the palace and a footman stepped forward to open the door and let down the steps. Even though Sunny had lived at Swindon for only a few months and that interval had been far from happy, she felt a surprising sense of homecoming.

It helped that the full glory of an English spring had arrived. All nature was in bloom, and the sun was almost as warm as high summer. As they entered the main hall, Sunny asked the butler, "Is my husband in the house or out on the estate?"

She assumed the latter, for Justin was not expecting them to return until the next day. But the butler replied, "I believe the duke is taking advantage of the fine weather by working in the Greek gazebo. Shall I inform him of your arrival?"

Sunny's heart lurched. She had thought she would have several hours more before confronting her husband about the state of their marriage, but perhaps it would be better this way. "No, I shall freshen up and then surprise him."

As she walked toward the stairs, a black-and-tan whirlwind darted across the hall and leapt against her, barking joyfully. "Daisy! Oh, darling, I missed you, too." Sunny knelt and hugged the little dog, feeling that such a warm welcome was a good omen.

A moment later, the wolfhounds thundered up and greeted Alexandra eagerly, then escorted her upstairs. Canine snobs of the highest order, they could tell aristocratic British blood from that of an upstart American, and they reserved their raptures for Justin and his sisters.

Sunny didn't mind. Her charming mongrel at her heels, she went to her room and changed from her traveling suit to her most flattering tea gown, a loose, flowing confection of figured green silk that brought out the green in her eyes.

She chose the costume with care, and not just because it was comfortable. The free and easy design of a tea gown was considered rather daring because it hinted at free and easy morals. She hoped Justin would see her garb as the subtle advance that it was.

Because he always seemed to like her hair, she let it down and tied it back with a scarf. She needed all the help she could get, for she was terrified by the prospect of baring her heart to the man who could so easily break it.

Apart from a brief note that she had written to inform Justin of their safe arrival in Paris, there had been no communication between them. For all she knew, he was still furious over Paul Curzon's kiss.

Fortunately, she had news that should mollify any lingering anger. God willing, it would also bring them together.

Chin high, she sailed out of the house and down the path toward the gardens.

❧

A breeze wafted through the miniature Greek temple, carrying exuberant scents of trees and spring flowers. Justin scarcely noticed. He was hardly more aware of the pile of correspondence that lay on the cushioned bench beside him, for thoughts of his wife dominated his mind. All of his grief, guilt and anguished love had been intensified by that night of heartbreaking passion, when he had briefly thought that their spirits and bodies were in total harmony.

Sunny had sent him a single impersonal note from Paris. Though it gave no hint of her feelings, its civility implied that she was willing to go on as if nothing had happened.

Yet he feared her return almost as much as he longed to see her. Having once found passion in her arms, it was going to be almost impossible for him not to try to invoke it again, whether she was willing or not.

Absently he slit an envelope with the Italian dagger he used as a letter opener. Before he could pull out the folded sheet inside, a soft voice said, "Good day, Justin."

He froze. Then he looked up to see Sunny poised on the edge of the folly, her right hand resting on one of the Ionic columns that framed the entrance. She wore a flowing green tea gown that made her look like an exquisite tree nymph. The garment was distractingly similar to a nightgown, and the breeze molded the fluttering, translucent layers of fabric to her slim figure.

For an instant all his tormented desire must have showed in his face. He wanted to cross the marble floor and draw her into his arms and never let her go. But he didn't. She looked ready to run if he made a move toward her, and it was unbearable to think that she might fear him.

He set the pile of letters on the bench beside him and courteously got to his feet. "I hope you had a good journey. I wasn't expecting you and Alex until tomorrow."

"Rather than spend another night in London, we decided to come home early."

"I'm glad. The house has seemed empty without the two of you."

Afraid to look at her because of what his expression would reveal, he turned the dagger over and over in his hands. The impact of her presence had driven away all of the eloquent, romantic speeches he had been rehearsing in his mind.

After a strained silence, she said, "I have good news. I'm almost certain that... that I am with child."

His first reaction was delight, but that was instantly shadowed by the implications. Augusta Vangelder had told him that once her daughter conceived, she was not to be troubled by husbandly lust. The fact that Sunny was brandishing the possibility of her pregnancy like a shield was clear proof that she welcomed the excuse to ban him from her bed.

His fingers whitened around the handle of the dagger. If she bore a son, her obligation to the Aubrey name would be fulfilled, and their marriage would effectively be over. Driving the dagger into his belly would have hurt less than that thought.

During the last lonely month, he had resolved to take advantage of the quiet intimacy of the marital bed to speak more openly to his wife. If she was willing, perhaps they could build a closer, warmer relationship. Now that hope was gone. Any discussions between them must endure the harsh light of day.

Knowing that the silence had been too long, he said, "Excellent. I hope you are feeling well?"

She nodded.

After another awkward pause, he said, "Good. We shall have to get a London physician here to make sure that your health is all it should be." He laid the dagger precisely on top of his correspondence so that the letters would not blow away in the wind. "You need not worry that I will continue to... force my attentions on you."

"Very well." She bent her head, and a slight shiver passed through her. Relief, perhaps. "I'm a bit tired. I think that I'll skip dinner and have a tray in my room."

Thinking that she looked pale, he said, "Of course. You must take good care of yourself." Back straight and head high, she turned and started down the grassy path. Every inch a lady, and as unapproachable as Queen Victoria herself.

He watched her leave, very aware of what an effort it was to breathe. Inhale, exhale. Inhale, exhale. He had been breathing all his life, yet never noticed before how difficult it was.

There was a tearing sensation deep inside, as if his heart was literally breaking. Unable to bear the deadly silence continue, he said in a voice that was less than steady, "Sunny?"

She halted, then turned slowly to face him. In the shadows cast by the tall boxwoods that lined the path, he could not see her face clearly.

He stepped from the folly and moved toward her, then stopped when she tensed. "Sunny, I want to apologize for what I did at Cottenham. I am profoundly sorry for distressing you."

"You were within your rights, and your anger was justified," she said expressionlessly.

"Perhaps, but that doesn't make it right to mistreat you. It won't happen again."

"Should I be grateful for that?" she said with sudden, chilling bitterness. "That night was upsetting, but it was also the one time in our marriage that you have shown any feelings about me. I have begun to think that even anger is better than indifference."

The gay ribbons on her gown shivered as she bowed her head and pressed her fingertips to her brow. When she looked up, her eyes were bleak. "We can't continue to live together as strangers, Justin. I can't endure it any longer."

Her words struck with the force of a blow, nearly destroying his fragile control. It seemed impossible that their marriage could be ending like this, on a day full of sunlight and promise. Yet he could not hold her against her will. Somehow he must find the strength to let her go. "If you wish to be free of me," he said tightly, "I will set no barriers in your way."

Her mouth twisted. "Is that what you want? To end our marriage now that you have your damned roof?"

"I want you to be happy, Sunny." Hearing the anguish in his voice, he stopped until he could continue more steadily. "And I will do anything in my power that might make you so."

The air between them seemed to thicken, charged with indefinable emotions. She broke the silence when she said passionately, "What I want is to be a real wife! To be part of your life, not just another expensive bauble in Swindon Palace." Her hands clenched at her sides. "Or perhaps I should wish to be your mistress, since English lords seem to save their hearts for women who are not their wives."

Stunned, he stammered, "I don't understand."

"It's a simple matter, Justin. I want you to love me," she said softly. "Do you think that you ever could? Because I'm horribly afraid that I love you."

He felt as if his heart had stopped. Her declaration was so unexpected that it seemed she must be mocking him. Yet it was impossible to doubt the transparent honesty in her eyes.

Before he could find the words to answer, her face crumpled and she spun away from him. "Dear God, I'm making a fool of myself, aren't I? Like the brash, vulgar American that I am. Please forget that I ever spoke."

Justin's paralysis dissolved and he caught her arm and swung her around before she could dart down the path. To his horror, tears were coursing down her face. The sight delivered a final, shattering blow to his reserve.

Crushing her in his arms, he said urgently, "Don't cry, Sunny! If you want my love, you already have it. You always have."

Though her tears intensified, she did not pull away. Instead, she wrapped her arms around him and hid her face in the angle between his throat and shoulder. She was all pliant warmth, honeyed hair and the promise of wild violets.

He groped for the best way to tell her how much he loved her until he realized that words had always failed and divided them. Action would better demonstrate the depth of his caring. He raised her head and brushed back her silky hair, then kissed her with all of the hunger of his yearning spirit.

Salty with tears, her lips clung to his, open and seeking. Subtle currents flowed between them. Despair and comfort, wonder and promise, trust and surrender. In the stark honesty of desperation, there was no place for shame or doubt or misunderstanding. One by one, the barriers that had divided them crumbled away to reveal the shy grandeur of love.

At first the sweetness of discovery was enough, but as the kiss deepened and lengthened, sweetness slowly blossomed into fire. Murmuring her name like a prayer, he kneaded the soft curves that lay unconstrained beneath her flowing gown. She pressed against him, breathless and eager, and he drew her down to the sun-warmed grass.

They had had dutiful conjugal relations, and once they had come together with chaotic, disquieting passion. This time, they made love.

She yielded herself utterly, for the awesome needs of her body no longer frightened her now that she knew she was loved. Rippling layers of green silk were easily brushed aside, buttons undone, ribbons untied.

Too impatient to wait until they were fully disrobed, they joined in the dance of desire. Swift and fierce, their union was a potent act of mutual possession that bound them into one spirit and one flesh.

Only afterward, as she lay languidly in the haven of his arms, did she realize the scandalousness of her behavior. The Duchess of Thornborough was lying half-naked in the garden, as bold as any dairymaid in a haystack.

How strange. How shocking. How right.

His head lay pillowed on her shoulder, and she slid her fingers into his tousled dark hair. "How is it possible for us to say so much to each other in ten minutes when we didn't speak a single word?" she asked dreamily.

"Words are limiting. They can only hint at an emotion as powerful as love. Passion comes closer because it is itself all feeling." Justin rolled to his side and propped himself up on one elbow, his other arm draped over her waist to hold her close. Smiling into her eyes, he said, "For someone who seemed to hate being touched, you have developed a remarkable talent for physical intimacy."

She blushed. "At first I was afraid of the unknown. It wasn't long until I began to look forward to your visits, but I was ashamed of my desire. My mother said that a man would never respect an immodest woman who reveled in her lower nature."

"In this area, your mother's understanding is sadly limited. There may be men like that but for me, the knowledge that we can share our bodies with mutual pleasure is the greatest of all gifts." He leaned over and dropped a light kiss on the end of her nose. "Let us make a pact, my love. We'll pay no attention to what the world might say, and care only about what the two of us feel."

With one hand, she unbuttoned the top of his shirt and slipped her fingers inside so she could caress his warm, bare skin. "I think that is a wonderful idea. I only wish that we had started sooner. I was so sure that you married me only because you needed my fortune."

Expression serious, he said, "Don't ever doubt that I love you, Sunny. I have since the first time we met, when you were the Gilded Girl and I was an insignificant younger son who could never dare aspire to your hand."

Her eyes widened. "We hardly even spoke that day."

"On the contrary. We walked through the gardens for the better part of an hour. I could take you along the exact route, and repeat everything you said. It was the most enchanting experience of my life." His mouth quirked up wryly. "And you don't remember it at all, do you?"

"I remember the gardens and that I enjoyed your company, but I was meeting so many people then. You were simply a quiet, attractive man who didn't seem interested in me." She looked searchingly into his eyes. "If you loved me, why didn't you say so sooner?"

"I tried, but you never wanted to hear." He began lazily stroking her bare arm. "Since it never occurred to me that you could love me, there was no reason to burden you with my foolish emotions, even if I had known how to do it."

A vivid memory of his proposal flashed through her mind. He had said then that she had had his heart from the moment they met. There had been other occasions when he had haltingly tried to declare himself, plus a thousand small signs of caring, from his wedding orchids to the way he had risked his life to rescue a puppy for her.

Yet because of her pain over Paul's betrayal and her conviction that Justin had married her only for money, she had spurned his hesitant words and gestures, convinced that they were polite lies. Dear heaven, no wonder he had preferred to conceal his feelings!

"I'm the one who must apologize. Because I was hurting, I ended up hurting you as well." She laid her hand along his firm jaw, thinking how handsome he looked with that tender light in his eyes. "Yet you were always kind to me."

He turned his head and pressed a kiss into her palm. "We gargoyles are known for kindness."

"I hate that nickname!" she said vehemently. "How can people be so cruel? You are intelligent amusing, considerate, and a gentleman in the best sense of the word."

"I'm very glad you think so, but society loves cleverness, and a good quip counts for more than a good heart," he said with dry amusement. "The fact that you love me is clear proof that much of love comes from simple proximity."

"Nonsense," she said tartly. "Proximity can just as easily breed dislike. But it's true that I would never have learned to love you if we hadn't married. You are not an easy man to know."

"I'm sorry, my dear." He sighed. "As you know, my mother can be difficult. I learned early that to show emotions was to risk having them used against me, so I became first-rate at concealing what I felt. Unfortunately, that left me at a flat loss at saying what matters most. I promise that from now on, I will say that I love you at least once a day."

"I'd rather have that than the Thornborough tiara." Shyly she touched her abdomen, which as yet showed no sign of the new life within. "Are you happy about the baby? You didn't seem very interested."

"I'm awed and delighted." A shadow crossed his face. "If my reaction seemed unenthusiastic, it was because I feared that if it was a boy, you would go off to Paris or New York and never want to see me again."

"What a dreadful thought!" She shivered. "May I ask a favor?"

"Anything, Sunny. Always." He laced his fingers through hers, then drew their joined hands to his heart.

"I would very much like it if we slept together every night, like people who can't afford two bedrooms do." Her mouth curved playfully. "Even with central heating, it's often chilly here."

He laughed, jubilant. "I would like nothing better! I've always hated leaving you to go back to my own cold and lonely bed."

"We can start a new fashion for togetherness." She lifted their clasped hands and lovingly kissed his fingertips.

He leaned over and claimed her mouth, and the embers of passion began glowing with renewed life. As he slid his hand into the loose neckline of her gown, he murmured, "We're both wearing entirely too many clothes, especially for such a fine day."

Remembering their surroundings, she said breathlessly, "Justin, don't you dare! We have already behaved disgracefully enough for one day."

"Mmm?" He pulled her gown from her shoulder so that he could kiss her breasts, a process that rendered her quite unable to talk. She had not known that there was such pleasure in the whole world.

She made one last plea for sanity as he began stripping

off his coat. "If someone comes along this path and sees us, what will they say?"

"They'll say that the Duke of Thornborough loves his wife very much." He smiled into her eyes with delicious wickedness. "And they'll be right."

Finis

AUTHOR'S NOTE

Thank you for taking the time to read *Weddings of the Century*. I hope you've enjoyed it—and if so, please consider helping other readers find it by leaving a review of the novel at your favorite online bookstore or reader website.

If you'd like to read more of my work, or if you want to see whether there are any books you've missed, the booklist which follows includes all of my titles which are currently available—and more are coming soon!

And if you'd like me to let you know when my upcoming books are published, you can join my newsletter by visiting my website at MaryJoPutney.com.

Happy reading!

—Mary Jo Putney

ALSO BY MARY JO PUTNEY

The Bargain

The Marriage Spell (paranormal)

Putney Classics (Sweet Regency Romances)

Carousel of Hearts

The Diabolical Baron

The Lackland Abbey Chronicles

(Young Adult fiction, written as M. J. Putney)

Dark Mirror, #1 (includes a bonus Lackland short story)

Dark Passage, #2

Dark Destiny, #3

The Guardian Trilogy

A Kiss of Fate, #1

Stolen Magic, #2

A Distant Magic, #3

The Lost Lords Series

Loving A Lost Lord, #1

Never Less Than A Lady, #2

Nowhere Near Respectable, #3

No Longer A Gentleman, #4

Sometimes A Rogue, #5

Not Quite A Wife, #6

Not Always a Saint, #7

Rogues Redeemed Series (A Spin-Off of the Lost Lords)

Once A Soldier, #1

Once a Rebel, #2

Once A Scoundrel, #3

Once A Spy, #4

Once Dishonored, #5

Once A Laird, #6

The Circle of Friends Trilogy

The Burning Point, #1

The Spiral Path, #2

An Imperfect Process, #3

A Holiday Fling (novella, also published in *Christmas Revels*)

Shorter Works

Weddings of the Century: A Pair of Novellas

The Christmas Cuckoo (novella, also published in *Christmas Revels*)

The Black Beast of Belleterre (novella, also published in *Christmas Revels*)

Sunshine for Christmas (novella, also published in *Christmas Revels*)

The Dragon and the Dark Knight (written as M.J. Putney)

Christmas Collections

Christmas Revels

Christmas Candles

Mischief and Mistletoe (contributor)

The Last Chance Christmas Ball (contributor)

Christmas Roses (contributor)

Seduction on a Snowy Night (contributor)

ABOUT THE AUTHOR

A *New York Times, Wall Street Journal,* and *USAToday* best-selling author, Mary Jo Putney is also a recipient of RWA's Nora Roberts Lifetime Achievement Award. She was born in Upstate New York with a reading addiction, a condition for which there is no known cure. Her entire romance writing career is an accidental byproduct of buying a computer for other purposes.

Her novels are known for psychological depth and intensity and include historical and contemporary romance, fantasy, and young adult fantasy. Winner of numerous writing awards, including two RITAs and two *Romantic Times* Career Achievement awards, she's had a number of her books listed as top romances of the year by *Library Journal* and *Booklist,* the magazine of the American Library Association.

You can visit her online at MaryJoPutney.com.

COPYRIGHT

PANDAMAX PRESS